W
of Sea

By
Sandra Forrester

© Copyright 2003 by Sandra Forrester
Illustrations © copyright 2003 by Barron's Educational Series, Inc.

Cover illustration and maps by Nancy Lane

All inquiries should be addressed to:
Barron's Educational Series, Inc.
250 Wireless Boulevard
Hauppauge, New York 11788
http://www.barronseduc.com

Library of Congress Catalog Card No.: 2003051872

International Standard Book No.: 0-7641-2633-4

PRINTED IN THE UNITED STATES OF AMERICA
9 8 7 6 5 4 3 2 1

Contents

Ollie's drawing of Sea-Dragon Bay

The Black Tower →

"Safe" Water

The Sandcastle

Legend: ✳ Sea Monster

⇧ Rip current

🔥 Firedrake

Island on the Edge

Ring of Sand

Sandbar

The Firedrake Inn

1

The Girl Who Knew Too Much

Beatrice Bailey was leaving Spanish class when she nearly bumped into a cluster of girls just outside the door. They were speaking in low voices, but their words came spilling out in a breathless rush. Beatrice picked up on their excitement even before she heard what they were saying.

"And how about that outfit?" Shannon Doolittle was demanding.

"Yeah. Looks like she came out in her underwear."

Beatrice grimaced at the sound of Amanda Bugg's voice, which was usually laced with malice and condescension, as it was now.

"She's the artsy type," Olivia Klink said. "From New York, maybe."

"More like Neptune," Amanda responded with a sneer.

"But you have to admit she's beautiful." Shannon gave Amanda a sly look. "Even your Jason couldn't take his eyes off her."

Uh-oh, Beatrice thought. *Shannon's in for it now.* And sure enough, just before Beatrice was swallowed up by the jostling stream of noisy middle schoolers who had surged into the hall, she caught a glimpse of Amanda's face turning a furious red.

Who in the world can they be talking about? Beatrice wondered as she made her way through the crowd to the stairs. She hadn't noticed a new girl in school, certainly no one who would stand out. And this girl, whoever she was, sounded intriguingly odd.

Beatrice, of course, wasn't privy to her classmates' gossip because they considered *her* beyond odd. Some of them liked nothing better than rehashing memories of Beatrice's peculiar behavior, insisting that she had to be a witch, while others, who rejected the notion of witches outright, tried to find other reasons to explain why Beatrice made them nervous. A few even felt vaguely guilty—because they had to admit, deep down, that Beatrice Bailey was one of the nicest people they knew.

Teddy Berry was already at their lockers when Beatrice arrived. The two girls were twelve years old and had been best friends since nursery school. Teddy was petite and pretty, with a tumble of short brown curls and dark eyes behind oversize wire-rim glasses. Beatrice was tall and skinny. Her pale red hair was cut straight across at the shoulder, with silky bangs that habitually fell into her green-gold eyes. People sometimes remarked that Beatrice's eyes and angular face gave her the appearance of an inquisitive cat. The comparison pleased her.

"Teddy, have you noticed anyone unusual around here lately?" Beatrice asked.

"Unusual how?" Teddy was digging through the jumble in her locker and appeared to have her mind on other things.

"Let's say . . . more unusual than you and me."

At this, Teddy gave Beatrice her full attention and grinned. "That unusual, huh? Well," she said, her gaze shifting to a spot just over Beatrice's left shoulder, "there's that girl over there. I'd say she's pretty unusual."

Beatrice turned around. There was no mistaking the girl Teddy meant. She was standing near the water fountain a few feet away. Other students peered at the girl as they passed but gave her plenty of space, as if they couldn't imagine shoving, elbowing, or bumping into *her*.

The girl was dressed completely in white, in soft, gauzy fabrics that would have been ideal for a hot summer day. But it was only March, and Beatrice shivered as her eyes traveled up from the bare sandals to the layered skirts that looked suspiciously like ruffled cotton petticoats to the sleeveless camisole that might have been an old man's undershirt to the lace-trimmed vest that covered it all. The girl wore several necklaces that fell in a tangle to her waist, all spun-silver ropes adorned with pearls and silver charms and tiny beads that glowed like rubies under the harsh fluorescent lights. As Beatrice had surmised, this new student was delightfully different from all the other kids in their uniform jeans and skirts bought at the same half-dozen stores in the mall.

But even if she had been dressed like everyone else, the girl would have been conspicuous. For one thing, she was tall—at least two inches taller than Beatrice—and nearly as thin. Except people would probably call her slender instead of skinny, because she was exquisitely beautiful and . . . Beatrice searched for the right word before finally settling on *sophisticated.*

"Do you know her name?" Beatrice asked Teddy, not taking her eyes off the girl in petticoats.

"Miranda Pengilly. When she walked into homeroom this morning, everybody stopped talking and just gawked at her." Teddy was studying Miranda with a tiny frown. "Pretty immature reaction, if you want my opinion."

Beatrice picked up on the jealousy in Teddy's voice and glanced sympathetically at her friend. After all, Teddy had always been the prettiest girl in school. *Weird,* by most peoples' estimation, but undeniably attractive. And suspected witch or not, the boys had been flirting with Teddy, and the girls admiring her cool clothes (albeit from a safe distance), for as long as Beatrice could remember. Things like that mattered to Teddy. But even more important to her than being the prettiest and the best dressed was her obsession with becoming the greatest witch who had ever lived. Teddy was ambitious.

"I mean, she's not *that* gorgeous," Teddy muttered.

Actually, she is, Beatrice thought.

Miranda Pengilly's features were perfect, and because of that, she could get away with wearing her black hair cut very short. In fact, the little-boy style was absolutely right for her. The smoky-lashed eyes were pale gray—almost the same color of silver as the chains around her neck—and were now gazing into the sea of curious, staring faces with an expression of bored indifference.

Beatrice stared right along with everyone else because she had never seen anyone like this girl before. Then, with

4

a start, Beatrice realized that the girl was staring back at her. And for the first time, there was a spark of interest in those coldly beautiful eyes.

Now the girl was walking toward Beatrice. Students stepped aside to let her pass. Beatrice's heart began to beat wildly against her ribs, and she felt a moment of confusion. Why had Miranda Pengilly picked her out from all the others? And why did the girl's approach feel so . . . *threatening*?

There was absolute silence. Everyone stood frozen, watching the new girl make her way steadily toward Beatrice. Watching her stop right in front of Beatrice.

Teddy inhaled sharply. Beatrice shifted uneasily as the girl's silver eyes found hers and held them. Then Miranda Pengilly said in a voice barely above a whisper, so that only Beatrice and Teddy could hear, "I want you to tell me about your magic. About how you broke Dally Rumpe's spells on Winter Wood and Werewolf Close. Have lunch with me and we'll talk."

Beatrice felt the blood drain from her face, and she thought for a moment that she was going to faint. How could this girl have heard about Winter Wood and Werewolf Close? The other kids might *suspect* Beatrice of being a witch, but—somehow—Miranda Pengilly *knew*!

Miranda's eyes lingered for a moment longer on Beatrice's stunned face. Then her lips curved into a smug half smile. She was obviously pleased with the reaction she had caused.

"I'll meet you outside the cafeteria," Miranda said, and walked away before Beatrice could respond.

Again, the crowd parted to let her pass. Then the buzzing started.

"Could you hear what she said?"

"Did you see Beatrice's face?"

Ignoring the stir around her, Beatrice turned to Teddy, who was staring after Miranda in disbelief.

"Who *is* she?" Teddy spoke softly, but her tone was urgent. "How could she possibly know?"

Beatrice shook her head and took a deep breath, waiting for her heart to stop pounding in her ears. She couldn't imagine how the girl had learned about their trips to the Witches' Sphere. But she had a sick feeling that she was going to find out.

Beatrice was aware of kids watching her more than usual as she walked down the hall to her next class. Everyone looked up when she entered the classroom, their eyes boring into her face. *Word spreads fast around here*, Beatrice thought grimly, and slid into a desk near the back.

While Mrs. Abel talked on and on about some battle, Beatrice's mind swirled with fears and questions. She was a witch living in the mortal world, and that wasn't always easy. For some reason, one of Beatrice's ancestors had left his life as a Traditional witch in the Witches' Sphere, shortened the family name of Bailiwick to Bailey, and come to live in this town as a modern Reform witch. From that day on, the Baileys had been forced to practice constant vigilance and secrecy. Beatrice had learned early that most mortals are suspicious of people who seem different from themselves—especially witches!—and she tried hard to fit in. As did her three friends, Teddy, Ollie, and Cyrus. But most of their classmates and neighbors seemed to sense right away that there was something uncanny about the four and their families. Only no one had been able to prove it—at least, not yet.

A chill crept over Beatrice as she remembered Miranda Pengilly's words. How could the girl have found out? And what did she want from Beatrice? Was she going to blackmail her? Beatrice's parents owned a successful nursery and garden center in town, but they were far from rich. If Miranda demanded a lot of money, what would they do?

The sad thing is, Beatrice thought now, *I'm not even a very* good *witch.* Like her parents and her three friends, Beatrice had only limited magical powers. *Extremely* limited. Which is why she had been so astonished when the Witches' Executive Committee had shown up on her twelfth birthday—*not* to give her the Everyday classification that she had expected, but to tell her that they planned to test her. If she could pass the test, she would be classified as a Classical witch, which meant they considered her capable of working important magic. Beatrice had never believed for a minute that she was anything more than an Everyday witch—nor did she especially *want* to be! But the Executive Committee didn't give her a choice, and as it turned out, Beatrice's own family history had provided the means to test her magical abilities. As the eldest female Bailiwick witch in her generation, Beatrice was charged with trying to break an ancient spell cast by the evil and powerful sorcerer, Dally Rumpe.

Beatrice's face turned pink with embarrassment when she recalled her first trip to the Witches' Sphere. She couldn't believe that she and her three friends had had the audacity to even *try* to reverse Dally Rumpe's spell. They had been so naive, not to mention *inept*! But with a lot of luck (Beatrice still believed that it was mainly luck that had seen them through), they had—miraculously!—managed to break Dally Rumpe's spell on Winter Wood. Two months later, they'd done the same in Werewolf Close.

But how did Miranda find out? Beatrice asked herself again. No one outside the Witches' Sphere would have any way of knowing.

And that's when it came to her! Beatrice gasped softly, but the kids around her heard and turned bright, expectant eyes in her direction. Beatrice didn't notice. She was oblivious to everything except the terrifying possibility that had suddenly taken hold in her mind.

She was remembering. The last time she saw Dally Rumpe. She had just repeated the words to break the spell, and the sorcerer's body was evaporating into a cloud of mist, and he had said to her right before he disappeared, *Next time, Beatrice Bailiwick, I won't wait for you to come to me.*

Beatrice closed her fingers around the edges of her history book to keep them from trembling. The sorcerer's words had alarmed her when he spoke them and she'd worried about them ever since. And now Spring Break would be starting in a few days, and the Witches' Executive Committee would probably be coming soon to tell them to return to the sphere for the third part of the test. *What if Dally Rumpe had followed Beatrice here to stop her? What if . . .* Beatrice's hands clenched the book so tightly that her knuckles turned white. *What if, this time, Dally Rumpe had disguised himself as a new girl in school? Could it be? Could it possibly be that Miranda Pengilly was Dally Rumpe?*

Beatrice leaped up from her desk, and the history book went crashing to the floor. Startled students jumped, then stared as Beatrice raced for the door. Mrs. Abel was calling her name, but Beatrice didn't hear. She flung open the door and started running down the hall.

At the bottom of the stairs, Beatrice screeched to a stop outside the art room. Through the window in the door, she could see Cyrus's dark head bent over a drawing. Teddy sat beside him, a charcoal pencil poised in the air as she gazed thoughtfully at the ceiling. Beatrice tapped lightly on the glass and Teddy's brown eyes slid to the door. Seeing Beatrice gesture for her to come, Teddy lowered her head toward Cyrus and said something. Then the two stood up and started for the door.

Mr. Wiggins asked where they were going, but Beatrice couldn't hear Teddy's response. When Teddy and Cyrus stepped out into the hall, the art teacher was right behind them.

"Let's get out of here," Beatrice said hastily.

They sprinted for the back door, then ran across the grassy field behind the school, stopping only when they reached the fence around the tennis courts.

"Okay, tell us," Cyrus said, panting. "What's happened?"

Cyrus Rascallion was small and dark, with vivid blue eyes. The good-natured grin that he normally wore was absent as he studied Beatrice's face with obvious concern.

Beatrice blew her bangs out of her eyes and took a deep breath. "All right. Do you remember Dally Rumpe's last words to me in Werewolf Close?"

"Not really," Teddy admitted.

"He said, 'Next time, Beatrice Bailiwick, I won't wait for you to come to me.'" Beatrice frowned. "I've had nightmares about those words. I don't know—maybe I'm overreacting—but I was trying to figure out how Miranda Pengilly knew about me—" She looked at Cyrus. "Oh—you weren't there, but this new girl—"

"Teddy told me," Cyrus said quickly. Then comprehension dawned on his face. "You don't think—Surely he wouldn't—"

"*What?*" Teddy demanded. "Are you guys speaking in some kind of code?"

"I'm wondering if Miranda Pengilly could be—"

Teddy started to nod her understanding. "Dally Rumpe," she finished softly. "That would explain how she knows so much about you. Only I don't think he'd come to the mortal world, do you? Does he have any power here?"

Beatrice shrugged. "I don't know." She paused, chewing nervously on her lip. "But what other explanation could there be? How could a mortal know about Winter Wood and Werewolf Close? What mortal has even *heard* of them? And I'm supposed to have lunch with her today!"

"That's out," Teddy said firmly. "You don't need to be anywhere near her until we find out who she is. Besides, we're having lunch with Ollie."

Ollie Tibbs was the only one of the four who didn't have to put up with nosy kids at school. Because he was home schooled. His family felt that public education—

with its emphasis on scientific theory and a mortal (meaning, *wrong*) slant on history—was a total waste of time for a witch. But Ollie's parents wanted him to have time to socialize with friends his own age, so Beatrice, Teddy, and Cyrus were often invited to lunch.

It was raining hard as they left school for Ollie's house.

"Forgot my umbrella," Teddy mumbled. She pulled her jacket up over her head and a gust of wind tugged at it. "My hair's going to be a mess all afternoon."

"No problem," Beatrice said, and began to chant:

Circle of magic, hear my plea,
Blowing winds,
Pesky rain,
This I ask you: make them flee.

As soon as Beatrice uttered the word *flee*, the rain ended and the wind stopped blowing.

"Thanks," Teddy said, lowering her jacket and shaking her curls. "I'm sure glad you can do weather spells."

"Too bad they're the *only* spells I can do," Beatrice replied dryly.

Ollie's house was only two blocks from school. It was big and white and rambling, looking a lot like Beatrice's, and for that matter, most of the other old houses in town. Except that witch houses—even those in the mortal world—are always a little different. Beatrice's house had lime-green shutters and colorful witch balls in the living room window. Ollie's house was less subtle. The weather vane, for instance, was a witch riding a broom. *That* had generated a few comments around town. And then there were the stepping-stones inscribed with witch sayings that led from the street to the front porch. Beatrice read them as she followed Teddy and Cyrus across the lawn. *As you harm none, do what you will . . . Bright blessings upon you . . . Merry meet, and merry part, and merry meet again.* The Tibbses had been asked to explain these more than once, as well.

Beatrice was wondering how anyone could find fault with such nice sentiments when her attention was drawn from the stones to the large cat sitting at the top of the porch steps. Longhaired and predominantly black, with dashes of orange and white, the cat was very beautiful. And very round.

"Cayenne!" Beatrice exclaimed, just as the front door opened. "What are you doing here?"

A tall, skinny boy with a mop of butter-yellow hair stepped out onto the porch and grinned, his green eyes twinkling. "I invited Cayenne for lunch. Word has it that you Baileys are starving her to death."

"The vet put her on a diet, Ollie." Beatrice looked unhappily at her cat. "I know she's a *little* plump, but I can't stand to see her pushing that empty bowl all over the kitchen floor. Okay, Cayenne, you can cheat just this once."

Apparently satisfied that she had Beatrice exactly where she wanted her, Cayenne leaped to her mistress's shoulder and rode purring into the house.

Beatrice had been coming to see Ollie for so many years, she barely noticed when the massive brown owl swooped down the front staircase to take their jackets in his beak. Nor did it startle her when the carpet runner on

12

which they were standing began to slide down the hall. As the runner approached a door in the rear wall, the door swung open by itself, and Beatrice and her friends found themselves in the kitchen. Ollie's father had once told Beatrice that owls and runners were cheaper than hiring a butler.

The Tibbses were an old, revered witch family, with more magic in their blood than most Reforms could ever hope for. So it was a source of deep frustration and humiliation to Ollie that the Tibbs gene for magic seemed to have skipped his generation. He was the only witch in his large extended family who couldn't cast a variety of complicated spells at will. In fact, the only spell he had mastered was making water boil.

Beatrice was dying to talk to Ollie about Miranda Pengilly. She asked for his advice all the time because he was smart and logical, and because he was very good at solving problems. The fact that he was also the most handsome boy she knew, and seemed to be developing a special interest in her, made his opinion matter even more.

But Ollie's mother was there, and Beatrice didn't want to mention Miranda in front of her. Mrs. Tibbs would probably get carried away and start casting spells to discover the girl's identity and intentions—and Mrs. Tibbs's spells weren't always discreet. Like the time she used magic to light candles in the dining room, only she didn't limit the spell to her *own* dining room, and candles were suddenly blazing all over town. Needless to say, the fire department was kept busy that night.

Mrs. Tibbs was standing at a counter that was covered with bowls of strange-looking mixtures. She was as fair and willowy as her son, with a narrow fine-boned face and pale hair that fell in a thick braid down her back. The dress she was wearing was long and silky and the color of ripe plums.

"Hi, Mrs. T," Cyrus said cheerfully. "You didn't have to go to all this trouble for us. A peanut butter and jelly sandwich is fine with me."

Mrs. Tibbs turned around and peered at Cyrus over her glasses. "I'm sure that would suit you," she said, trying to look stern. "You have the taste buds of a mortal, Cyrus. But I can assure you that you won't find that wretched peanut butter concoction in my house. And *this*," she added, waving a delicate hand toward the assorted mixing bowls, "has nothing to do with you. Mr. Tibbs and I are having a party tonight. A masquerade ball, in fact."

Teddy's face lit up. "Really? You always give the best parties, Mrs. Tibbs. But I didn't know . . ."

"That's because you weren't invited," Mrs. Tibbs responded amicably. "The ball is in honor of an old friend from the Witches' Sphere. Adults only."

"Oh." Teddy's face fell. She loved parties.

Just then, Beatrice noticed that one of Mrs. Tibbs's black dangling earrings appeared to be crawling down her neck. "Uh—Mrs. Tibbs—your earring seems to be getting away."

Mrs. Tibbs frowned. "Darn dragonflies. They're quite striking, I think, but they refuse to sit still."

"I like them," Teddy said. "They're even prettier than the caterpillars you had on last week."

"Well, sit down, all of you," Mrs. Tibbs told them. "I'll have lunch ready in a jiff."

As Beatrice and her friends gathered around the big kitchen table, cupboard doors and cabinet drawers began to fly open. Plates, cups, napkins, and silverware flew across the room and arranged themselves in attractive place settings on the table. The last piece to arrive was a covered casserole dish that landed lightly in the center.

Cyrus—who preferred a juicy hamburger and fries to witch food any day—peered suspiciously at the dish. "What is this, anyway?" he asked.

"Centipede casserole," Mrs. Tibbs said briskly. "Lots of calcium and protein for growing bones and muscles. And this," she added, sliding a plate in front of Cayenne, "is fennel tuna with lavender. For the girl on a diet."

Cayenne took a bite and promptly began to purr. A second bite, and the purr began to sound like a small leaf blower.

"So, Beatrice," Mrs. Tibbs said as she stirred a pot on the stove, "has the Witches' Executive Committee notified you about your next trip to the Sphere?"

Beatrice knew that Ollie's mother had more than a casual interest in her answer. The Tibbs had been devastated when Ollie was classified Everyday on his twelfth birthday. There hadn't been an Everyday witch in their family for a hundred years. But when Ollie had volunteered to help Beatrice break Dally Rumpe's spell, the Executive Committee had agreed to reconsider his classification. As well as Teddy's and Cyrus's.

Ollie gave Beatrice a sheepish look and shrugged.

"No, Mrs. Tibbs, not yet," Beatrice said. She scooped up a bite of casserole on her fork. It looked like bright yellow custard with some squiggly black things in it. *That must be the centipedes*, Beatrice decided. It smelled delicious.

"So what's the holdup?" Mrs. Tibbs demanded. "Don't they usually have you go during mortal school breaks? And isn't a break coming up in a few days?"

"Yes, ma'am," Beatrice replied. She chewed and swallowed. *Pretty good*, she thought. "But you know the committee," Beatrice said. "They always wait till the last minute."

Mrs. Tibbs sighed. And Ollie relaxed a little.

"Oliver," his mother said, "I forgot the catmint tea. Why don't you brew some for your friends?"

Ollie filled a kettle with water and began to chant:

> *Heat of flame, heat of fire,*
> *Give to me my one desire.*
> *Boil this water, bubbling free,*
> *As my will, so mote it be!*

The pot of water began to boil.

Cyrus had taken a tiny bite of the casserole and was looking ill. "Mrs. T, do you have some crackers? Or maybe a slice of old bread?"

Everyone laughed, even Mrs. Tibbs. "Cyrus," she said, "are you quite certain that you're a witch?"

After her last class, Beatrice went to her locker to get the books she needed for homework that night. She had just slammed the door shut when she became aware of someone standing behind her, watching. Even before she turned around, Beatrice knew who it would be.

"So," Miranda Pengilly said as Beatrice slowly faced her. "You made other plans for lunch, I take it. I'm not used to being stood up."

The girl's expression was neutral, but there was no mistaking the displeasure in her voice. The prospect of her anger left Beatrice feeling uneasy. For a moment, Beatrice considered coming up with an excuse, but then she balked. Wasn't she free to have lunch with anyone she wanted? She didn't have to answer to this girl.

Beatrice steeled herself and looked straight into Miranda Pengilly's pale gray eyes. "Who *are* you?" she asked.

"You don't need to know that yet," Miranda replied. There was that half smile again—amused, superior, and designed to intimidate. "You'll find out once we reach the Witches' Sphere. You see, I'll be going with you."

2

Masquerade Ball

"Why don't you call Ollie and tell him to come over?" Cyrus suggested. "We need to talk about that Miranda girl."

Beatrice, Teddy, and Cyrus had just turned onto Beatrice's street. All three appeared gloomy.

Beatrice glanced around nervously as they walked across her yard to the house. "Maybe I'm just anxious, but I think somebody's watching us."

"I'll find out," Teddy said, and began to chant:

> Candle, bell, and willow tree,
> Who does snoop and spy on me?
> Use your magic for our side,
> Show us who would wish to hide.

Suddenly, the azalea bushes in the yard across the street sprang apart, revealing a round-faced little boy with a startled expression.

"Oh," Beatrice said, looking relieved. "That's just Chester Sidebottom. He's always spying on us and carrying tales to his parents." Beatrice grinned and waved at the boy, who scrambled to his feet and sped around the side of the house.

"I'll call Ollie," Beatrice said as they trooped up the steps to the porch. "Then we'll have a snack."

Cayenne was sleeping in a basket reserved for mail on the hall table. She opened one green-gold eye when she heard Beatrice's voice, then yawned and stretched, scattering letters to the floor in the process.

"She heard the word *snack*," Cyrus said with a grin.

As if on cue, Cayenne leaped to Beatrice's shoulder to be carried to the kitchen.

A few minutes later, Ollie found the four of them there eating peanut butter sandwiches—at Cyrus's request. Cayenne was looking grumpy because Beatrice was only giving her tiny bites, and not many of those. Cyrus appeared blissful as he chewed.

Ollie sat down across from Beatrice, but he didn't touch the sandwich she placed in front of him. "I've been thinking all the way over here about what you told me on the phone," he said, his expression as serious as Beatrice had ever seen it. "You say this girl just showed up today?"

"Out of the blue," Teddy said before Beatrice could reply. "But I don't think we need to worry about her going with us. The Witches' Executive Committee would never let a mortal into the Sphere."

"That's true," Beatrice said, perking up a little. Then she frowned. "But that wouldn't keep her from blackmailing us. She could tell everybody at school what we've been doing."

"So what?" Teddy said. "Not even Amanda Bugg and that dopey boyfriend of hers would believe the truth. I mean, these kids have zero imagination. If Miranda starts filling their ears with stories about dragons and were-wolves, do you really think they're going to buy it?"

"Teddy has a point," Ollie said. "I think you should just ignore the girl."

"She's pretty hard to ignore," Beatrice protested, but she was feeling better.

"All I can say," Teddy said fiercely, "is she'd better not mess up my chance to be reclassified."

Beatrice and Ollie looked at each other and smiled. From Teddy's point of view, blackmail and danger paled beside someone standing in her way of becoming a Great Witch.

About that time, they heard a car pull up out front.

"Mom and Dad," Beatrice said. "I'll bet they brought Mexican food. We had hamburgers last night, and Chinese the night before. Do you guys want to stay? They always bring enough for twenty."

"I'd like to," Ollie said, "but my mom wants me home to meet her guests." He smiled ruefully. "Before I'm banished to my room."

"That's right, I'd forgotten about the ball," Teddy said wistfully. "Who's the guest of honor your mother mentioned?"

"His name is Noah Halfacre," Ollie said. "I've never met him."

"Noah Halfacre?" Cyrus sat straight up in his chair. "The *explorer*?"

"Yeah," Ollie said without much interest. "I think my mom said something about him climbing mountains and making maps and stuff."

"He's done a lot more than make maps!" Cyrus's face was flushed and his eyes sparkled neon blue. "He's spent years uncovering the route King Arthur traveled when he was still a kid studying under Merlin. Merlin the Magician," he added, glancing at Teddy.

"I *know* who Merlin is," Teddy said crossly. "Do you think I never read?"

"Anyway," Cyrus continued, "Noah Halfacre has been to all the dangerous, magical places Arthur visited with Merlin. He's the bravest explorer in the Sphere!"

Ollie shrugged. "I don't know anything about that. I just know that he's an old friend of the family."

"Ollie," Cyrus said, his expression intense as he leaned closer, "I *have* to meet him. Or at least *see* him. Noah Halfacre is my hero!"

"No kidding," Teddy muttered. Then something seemed to occur to her, and she looked quickly at Cyrus. "You know, it's always been *my* dream to meet Noah what's-his-name, too. Isn't that a coincidence?"

Beatrice laughed. "You just want to go to the ball."

"Sorry," Ollie said, grinning at Teddy. "But no kids are allowed. My parents would ground me for a month if they saw you two waltz in."

"They don't *have* to see us," Cyrus said, squirming in his chair as a plan formed in his mind. "I can shrink us, Ollie, and we'll hide in your pocket when you go to meet the guests. No one will know we're there."

"Are you nuts?" Ollie demanded. "Forget it."

"Ollie, *please*."

Cyrus looked like he might start to cry any minute and Beatrice felt sorry for him. She had never seen easygoing Cyrus this worked up.

"You know, Ollie," Beatrice said thoughtfully, "going to a masquerade ball does sound like fun. What harm could it do?"

Ollie spread his hands wide in a gesture of futility. "You're all nuts," he muttered. "It's the sad truth—my three best friends are completely *insane!*"

"I think that's a yes," Teddy said, and giggled.

Ollie didn't have time to respond because Mr. and Mrs. Bailey were coming through the kitchen door from the dining room carrying bags of Mexican food. Ollie raised his eyebrows at Beatrice and she grinned. "I know the schedule," she said.

Mr. and Mrs. Bailey were both tall and skinny like their daughter, and Mrs. Bailey had the same pale red hair.

"Well, if it isn't the fiendish four." Mrs. Bailey looked fondly at them and then bent down to kiss the top of Beatrice's head. "I hope you're all hungry."

Cyrus was eagerly sniffing the air.

Watching him, Ollie rolled his eyes. "I thought you just *had* to be someplace else tonight," he said pointedly.

"We have time for one enchilada," Cyrus replied. "Or two. I'll eat fast."

They hadn't taken their first bite when there was a knock on the back door. Which surprised everyone, since neighbors didn't just drop by the Baileys' for a friendly chat. But before anyone could respond, the door swung open and a dark head popped in.

It was all Beatrice could do to keep from saying, *Oh, no*, when she saw that it was Sasha Leake, one of several reporters from the Sphere who had been pestering Beatrice since her return from Werewolf Close. The Baileys had hoped they were finally rid of them. But obviously not.

The reporter came bouncing into the room, a small, energetic little witch in baggy khaki pants, with gelled hair sticking up in spikes and big hoop earrings. She was cute. She was persistent. And she was a pain in the neck.

"Hi, folks," Sasha said brightly. "Hope this isn't a bad time."

Beatrice could tell from her parents' expressions that they were as dismayed to see the reporter again as she was. Even Cayenne backed off from the scent of food and glared at Sasha. Probably because every time the reporter showed up, she shoved a camera lens into Cayenne's face and called her *Pudgy Kitty*.

"Uh—what brings you back this way, Sasha?" Mr. Bailey asked. "You got your interview with Beatrice— actually, *several* interviews with all of us. We've told you everything there is to know about our daughter, and she filled you in on what happened in the Witches' Sphere—"

"Yes, you've all been so patient and kind," Sasha chirped. "But when I started writing my story, I realized that it wasn't going to be any different from all the *other* stories written about Beatrice's defeat of Dally Rumpe."

"Actually," Beatrice said, trying to conceal her irritation, "*I* didn't defeat anyone. My *friends* and I worked together to break the spell."

"Exactly!" Sasha exclaimed. She pulled out a chair and scooted in between Beatrice and Mrs. Bailey, knocking a taco out of Beatrice's hand with her elbow. "So I need to talk with your friends, as well."

Teddy's face lit up. "I'd be happy to give you an interview. I'm Teddy Berry, Beatrice's best friend."

"*One* of Beatrice's best friends," Cyrus corrected, and scowled at Teddy. "But we don't have time to talk right now. We have—a previous engagement."

Sasha's whole body sagged. "It's just that this piece is so important to me," she said, her voice trembling a little. "I guess I'd better tell you all the truth." She dropped her eyes and looked embarrassed as she added, "I haven't been able to *distinguish* myself at the paper yet. Quite honestly, I don't think they're planning to keep me around much longer."

Hearing this, Beatrice felt a twinge of sympathy for the woebegone reporter. Even Mr. and Mrs. Bailey's expressions had softened.

"So, you see," Sasha went on hurriedly, "if I could come up with a great story—and a group of young Reform witches overthrowing Dally Rumpe is the *best* story of the year—I could save my job. And maybe," the reporter added longingly, "people would even start taking me seriously as a journalist."

No one spoke for a moment. Then Beatrice said, against her better judgment, "Well, I guess we can answer a few more questions."

"But not without some ground rules," Mr. Bailey said firmly. "You aren't to go through our medicine cabinet again."

"No, sir," Sasha vowed, attempting to look serious, but unable to hide her joy.

"Or the refrigerator," Mrs. Bailey added. "And you absolutely are not allowed to sift through our garbage."

"It won't happen again," Sasha said quickly, shaking her head earnestly and bouncing around a little in her excitement. "No way."

"And we can't talk to you tonight," Cyrus said, looking anxiously at the clock on the wall.

"That's right," Beatrice cut in as Sasha's mouth opened to protest. "How about tomorrow after school?"

"Tomorrow will be fine," Sasha replied, subdued now and actually sitting still. "And I promise to write a fantastic story. Every fact, every quote, will be accurate. Just call me Sasha Leake, Reporter of Truth."

Beatrice ducked her head to hide a smile.

"There's just one more thing," Sasha said.

"What is it?" Beatrice asked warily.

"I want to go with you on your next trip to the Sphere."

Beatrice and her friends' eyes met. *Boy,* Beatrice thought, *this trip is becoming more popular than Disney World.*

"I have a press pass," Sasha went on doggedly, "so I can leave and enter the Sphere whenever I want. I'll tag after you, if I have to. But if I could go with you," she said, her eyes pleading, "and get the story from the inside—"

"Okay, okay." Beatrice was tired of arguing. "I don't care, as long as it's all right with the Witches' Executive Committee."

"Oh, Beatrice, *thank you!*" Sasha clapped her hands like a child, happiness radiating from her smile and her eyes and her very pores. And she was bouncing in her chair again. "Really. You won't even know I'm there."

Right, Beatrice thought. *That will be the day.*

They stood behind a thick screen of cherry laurels in Ollie's yard. Cyrus held on to Beatrice and Teddy's hands while he chanted:

> By the mysteries, one and all,
> Make us shrink from tall to small.
> Cut us down to inches three,
> As my will, so mote it be.

Instantly, Cyrus, Beatrice, and Teddy began to shrink smaller and smaller, until they were only three inches tall. Ollie stooped so that they could step into his hand, and then placed them gently into the pocket of his jacket.

"I'm crazy to let you talk me into this," Ollie grumbled as he opened the door to his house.

By standing on her tiptoes, Beatrice could just see over the top of Ollie's pocket. The downstairs rooms were lit only by candles, pyramids of flickering flames leaping and cowering against pools of deep shadow. And through the shadows moved figures that might have just stepped out of a Renaissance play: men wearing dark velvet tunics and sweeping cloaks that brushed the floor when they walked; women in gowns of brightly colored silk, their hair swept up under strange-looking headpieces adorned with glittering stones. Some of the guests held masks on sticks, using them to cover the upper portions of their faces. Others had laid the masks aside and were eating and dancing with an abandon for which witches are famous.

"*Whoa!*" Teddy whispered in Beatrice's ear. "Can you believe these clothes?"

"Do you see anyone who looks like an explorer?" Cyrus asked in Beatrice's other ear.

Ollie had walked into the living room, where most of the guests were congregated. Beatrice caught a glimpse of Mrs. Tibbs, dressed in a shimmering yellow gown, with what appeared to be pale yellow moths clinging to her earlobes. When she heard Mrs. Tibbs call her son's name, Beatrice slipped down deeper into Ollie's pocket.

While Ollie was introduced to his parents' guests, Beatrice, Teddy, and Cyrus waited quietly, and not too comfortably. Their nest in Ollie's jacket was growing warmer by the minute, and the sounds of party chatter and music were painfully loud to their diminutive ears. Then they heard the name *Noah Halfacre*, and Cyrus scrambled to his feet. Teddy just yawned, but Beatrice stood up to look.

A small man with a graying goatee and very little hair on top of his bony head was standing between Mrs. Tibbs and a plump woman in red silk. He looked sort of mousy to Beatrice, and she wondered if Cyrus was disappointed by his hero. But then the explorer began to speak. He had a deep authoritative voice, and Beatrice realized right away that Noah Halfacre wasn't short on self-confidence.

"Of course, others have mapped Arthur's travels with Merlin," the man was saying, "but their accounts were grossly inaccurate, based more on legend than scholarly research. And most of them didn't actually bother to travel to the enchanted sites."

"But you went there, didn't you, Noah?" Mrs. Tibbs said.

"To each and every one!" the explorer exclaimed. "It was the great Merlin himself who said that you must see all and experience all if you are to fully understand. So, of course, I had to go."

"It must have been dangerous," the woman in red silk said with a touch of awe in her voice.

"But what an adventure, if one is willing to confront the dangers," Noah Halfacre replied, sounding quite satisfied with himself. "The ghosts on Haunted Mountain weren't pleased by my presence, I can assure you. And the songspells in the Hall of Shells threatened to lure me into the Land of the Beyond. And . . ."

Beatrice sat down next to Teddy and thought about taking a nap. But Cyrus was still peering out of the pocket at Noah Halfacre, hanging on to the explorer's every word.

"This isn't exactly what I expected," Teddy whispered. "I want *out* of here!"

Beatrice couldn't agree more. She was wishing she had a straight pin so that she could get Ollie's attention when she realized that they were moving again. The party sounds grew more and more distant, and then Ollie was reaching into his pocket to lift them out.

From the palm of Ollie's hand, Beatrice looked around and saw that they were in Mr. Tibbs's study at the back of the house.

"Have you had enough?" Ollie asked.

"Yes," Beatrice said.

"*No!*" This came from Cyrus. "You left right in the middle of Noah Halfacre telling about his adventure in The Place of Hanging Stones!"

"Ollie, I didn't think I'd be spending the whole evening in your pocket," Teddy said. "Take us someplace where we can see what's happening."

"I said I'd bring you and I have," Ollie replied, "but it's time to go. If you start wandering around on your own, we're in trouble."

"We'll stay in one place," Cyrus assured him.

"How about the bookshelves by the fireplace?" Teddy suggested. "It's dark there. No one will see us."

Ollie sighed and thought about it. "All right," he said finally, "I'll give you ten more minutes. But promise that you'll stay put—and if anyone comes over that way, dive behind the books."

"We promise," Teddy said happily. "But make that twenty minutes."

Ollie frowned at her before placing the three inside his pocket again. He headed back to the living room, where Beatrice heard Mrs. Tibbs say, "Don't you have homework to finish, Oliver?"

"I just needed to get a book," Ollie answered.

A moment later, Ollie's fingers slipped into his pocket, and Beatrice, Teddy, and Cyrus climbed into his cupped palm.

"Ten minutes," Ollie whispered, and placed them in a dark corner of the bookshelves.

Beatrice realized that Teddy had been right: No one was likely to notice them here, and they had a great view of the room.

Ollie reached for a book and pretended to look through it, while the other three enjoyed the show. A four-piece band was playing lively tunes that Beatrice recognized from their trips to the Witches' Sphere. And there was a mime with his face painted white—then Beatrice did a double take and saw that the mime was actually a vampire. The white face was natural.

More puzzling was the little girl in a red cape who moved from guest to guest with her very large gray dog.

"What's the kid with the dog doing here?" Beatrice whispered.

Ollie glanced up from his book. "Oh, that's Little Red Riding Hood."

"*The* Little Red Riding Hood?"

"Yep." Ollie smirked. "And that *dog* is a wolf."

As Red Riding Hood and her furry companion moved closer, Beatrice heard Red saying things to the guests like, "My, what big ears you have," while everyone largely ignored her. The wolf hunkered down in the middle of the dance floor to scratch at some fleas.

"Not a big hit," Beatrice remarked.

Ollie shrugged. "Fairy-tale characters are pretty old hat these days, so they work parties for practically nothing. See that little guy over there?"

Beatrice followed Ollie's gaze and saw a small man with a long tangled beard. He was stomping his foot and glaring at a guest while shouting, "Guess my name! Guess my name!"

"Don't tell me," Beatrice said.

Ollie grinned. "If you guess Rumpelstiltskin, you'll be right."

The little man stomped harder and yelled louder.

"Not exactly the life of the party, is he?" Beatrice mused.

"It's that Red Riding Hood that gets me," Teddy said. "She can't be too bright. I mean, she couldn't tell the difference between her grandmother and a *wolf*?"

Ollie replaced the book on the shelf and glanced at his watch. "You have one more minute, Teddy."

"*Wait*," Teddy said. "Look at those people who just came in. Beatrice, can you believe that gown?"

Beatrice glanced without much interest at the couple standing in the entrance to the living room. Both were tall, dark, and elegant. The woman's cream-colored gown was dazzling. But what instantly caught Beatrice's attention was a third person standing slightly behind them. A girl who was also tall and dark. She was wearing a pale gray gown and holding a gray-feathered mask over her eyes. But even with half her face concealed, Beatrice recognized the girl.

Mrs. Tibbs went over to greet the new arrivals, and the girl lowered her mask. *Yes*, Beatrice thought, her whole body tensing, *it's her*. The girl was Miranda Pengilly!

"Beatrice," Teddy hissed. "Do you see who that is?"

Beatrice nodded woodenly. Her mind wasn't working too well at the moment, but she did understand that the Tibbses wouldn't have invited these people to the ball unless they were witches.

Teddy was thinking the same thing. "Then Miranda isn't a mortal at all. She's a witch!"

Ollie jerked his head around to look at Beatrice. "That's Miranda Pengilly?"

"Yes," Beatrice said, "and your parents must know her. Can you find out who she is?"

"I'll try," Ollie answered, and started toward his mother, who had moved on to speak to other guests.

The elegant couple joined a group of witches on the other side of the room. Miranda tagged after them, looking out of sorts. She obviously didn't want to be there. Then a young male witch asked her to dance and Miranda's sulky expression vanished. She was smiling and animated as the young man led her out to the dance floor.

"This is unbelievable," Beatrice muttered.

"I thought kids weren't allowed," Cyrus grumbled. "How come *she's* invited?"

When Ollie came back, he said, "I'm in trouble. My mom said to get the books I need and split. *Now.*"

"But what about Miranda?" Beatrice demanded.

"Mom doesn't know her," Ollie said softly. "But those are Miranda's parents, Willow and Ephraim Pengilly. Ephraim's father was Donato Pengilly, the writer. Have you ever read *The Old Witch and the Sea* or *Lord of the Bats*? They won all kinds of awards in the Sphere."

Beatrice wasn't in the mood to discuss literature. "What else does your mother know about the family?" she asked impatiently.

"Willow and Ephraim just moved from the Witches' Sphere," Ollie said. "They had some kind of business that failed and they're hoping to do better here. Mom doesn't know anything else about them, and neither does Dad. He met Donato a few times at parties in the Sphere. That's the only reason the Pengillys were invited tonight."

Miranda and her partner had danced close enough for Beatrice to hear them talking.

"I'll be leaving town soon," Miranda was saying.

"That's too bad," the male witch responded.

Miranda's laugh was harsh, without humor. "Hardly," she said. "I'm wasting time. I need to go back home and take care of business."

Then they moved away, and Beatrice couldn't hear any more.

What kind of business? Beatrice wondered. She would have given a lot to know. Her life might depend on it.

Thirteen Witches

Teddy was spending the night with Beatrice to celebrate the start of Spring Break. They were in their pajamas and robes watching old movies on TV and eating pizza. The box was open on the coffee table and Cayenne was sitting in the lid snaring anchovies with her claws.

"I wish the Witches' Executive Committee wouldn't keep us waiting every time," Teddy complained. "They just show up whenever they feel like it and tell us we're leaving. I need time to pack."

"Maybe they've decided to stop the test," Beatrice said. "It must be obvious by now that we don't have an aptitude for magic."

"Bite your tongue," Teddy drawled. "We broke two parts of the spell, didn't we?"

"Luck," Beatrice said.

"Talent," Teddy countered. Then she looked at Beatrice with a puzzled expression. "Why is it that you don't want to be a Classical witch?"

"Because I like my life the way it is." Beatrice paused, then added, "I'm glad we were able to reverse Dally Rumpe's spell in Winter Wood and Werewolf Close, but,

Teddy, I know I'm never going to have extraordinary powers. I don't deserve a Classical classification. And if I had it, I wouldn't know what to do with it."

"You could do lots of things," Teddy insisted. "They'll send you to a witch academy and you'll learn lots of magic. Then, who knows? Maybe you'll go to work at the Witches' Institute. You might even end up on the Witches' Executive Committee."

Beatrice grimaced. "I don't think I'm executive material."

"Then you could teach at Witch U." Teddy was beginning to sound exasperated. "Or go on the lecture circuit. Beatrice, your problem is you don't have enough confidence in yourself. You need to start thinking big!"

Teddy went back to watching the movie, leaving Beatrice to ponder what she had said. Beatrice didn't think she had a problem with self-confidence. She was just being realistic. *Wasn't she?*

Beatrice was still lost in thought when the clock in the hall struck twenty-four. Midnight. Beatrice glanced over at Teddy and saw that she had fallen asleep. Cayenne was curled up against Teddy's back snoring gently.

Beatrice was about to rouse them when she noticed light spilling into the darkened room. At first, Beatrice thought her mother had come downstairs and turned on the hall light. Then she saw it: a large luminous orb floating through the doorway into the living room.

"Here we go again," Beatrice muttered. "Teddy," she said, "wake up. The Witches' Executive Committee is here."

Teddy opened her eyes just as the ball of light exploded. She screamed at the shower of shooting stars and ribbons of fire. Cayenne woke with a start, then dove under the sofa.

"Oh, it's them," Teddy said groggily, and began to comb her curly hair with her fingers. "I wish I were dressed better."

Beatrice sighed.

The first time the Witches' Executive Committee had appeared so dramatically, Beatrice had been astonished. Not to mention, frightened. But she knew what was coming now, and their sudden appearance only made her feel slightly nauseous.

Beatrice turned off the TV, pulled on her fuzzy green dragon slippers, and waited—as thirteen witches materialized in the middle of her living room.

Each witch held a candle that illuminated the rich colors of their jewel-tone robes and pointed hats. Only one of them was dressed in black. That was Dr. Thaddeus Thigpin, Director of the Witches' Institute. Candle light shimmered on his white hair and cast shadows across his gaunt, scowling face.

Dr. Thigpin had made it clear that he saw no benefit in testing a lowly Reform witch before classifying her. In fact, he found it an absolute waste of his time. Beatrice knew that he, at least, had no illusions about her magical potential.

Then Beatrice caught sight of her two favorite witches, Drs. Featherstone and Meadowmouse. Both were smiling at her, and Beatrice smiled back.

Dr. Thigpin stepped forward and glared at her, his ice-blue eyes narrowing under bushy white brows. "Well, Beatrice Bailiwick, we're together again."

As Beatrice had expected, he didn't sound happy about it.

"It's time for the third part of your test," Dr. Thigpin continued, his commanding voice sounding weary. "Dr. Featherstone and Dr. Meadowmouse will run through the particulars with you. Although I wonder why they bother," he added irritably. "By now, you can surely recite this part by heart."

Dr. Meadowmouse had come forward. "It's required that we explain it all to her, Thaddeus. Before each part of the test."

"Well, get on with it then," Dr. Thigpin snapped. "I'm an old witch and I need my rest."

Beatrice thought she saw Dr. Meadowmouse wink at her. He was such a dear! With his long, genial face and cap of shining brown hair that stood out from his head like a toadstool, Dr. Leopold Meadowmouse was one of the most gentle and considerate witches Beatrice had ever met.

But it was Dr. Featherstone that Beatrice knew best. Recently, Beatrice had learned that Aura Featherstone and Beatrice's mother had been close friends when they were young. Now Dr. Featherstone was taking a special interest in Nina Bailey's daughter. Beatrice was pretty sure that it was Dr. Featherstone who had persuaded the others to test her.

Dr. Featherstone had come to stand beside Dr. Meadowmouse. The thirty-something witch was extremely attractive, with hazel eyes that seemed to miss nothing and auburn hair spilling over the shoulders of her green silk robes. She turned around now to the other witches.

"Peregrine," Dr. Featherstone said, "are you there?"

A small man in mole brown robes disengaged himself from the cluster of witches and came forward shyly. Peregrine was Beatrice's witch adviser, and always accompanied Beatrice and her friends on their trips to the Witches' Sphere. He had very large ears that stuck out through his toast-colored hair and a small mouth that drooped at the corners. Now he gave Beatrice a tentative, crooked smile before ducking his head.

About that time, Mr. and Mrs. Bailey appeared in the doorway. Beatrice's mother was hastily tying the belt to her robe, and Beatrice's father was yawning.

"Come in, Nina," Aura Featherstone said cheerfully. "You, too, Hamish. We were just about to begin."

Dr. Meadowmouse was looking at a thick black book that lay closed on the desk. The book suddenly lifted into the air and sailed across the room, landing in his hands.

"*The Bailiwick Family History*," Dr. Meadowmouse said with satisfaction. "I always enjoy delving into this book. Fascinating reading."

"Can you just read it, please?" Dr. Thigpin barked.

Dr. Meadowmouse glanced benignly at the older witch. "Certainly, Thaddeus. But first, I am required by witch law to tell Beatrice the history that relates to our being here."

"If you must," Dr. Thigpin grumbled.

"Beatrice, as you know," Dr. Meadowmouse began, "you are descended from a very good and powerful sorcerer named Bromwich of Bailiwick, who is held captive by the evil sorcerer Dally Rumpe."

"Good grief!" Dr. Thigpin exclaimed. "She hardly needs to be told about Dally Rumpe. She *has* come up against him twice now."

"And won," Aura Featherstone pointed out pleasantly, to no one in particular.

Dr. Thigpin scowled at her.

"And you *know*," Dr. Meadowmouse continued without skipping a beat, "that two hundred years ago, Dally Rumpe cast a spell to gain control of the kingdom of Bailiwick. Only it backfired, and the kingdom was split into five parts. Dally Rumpe's spell upset the delicate balance of the four basic elements needed to sustain life."

"Earth, air, water, and fire," Beatrice said.

"*Exactly*." Dr. Meadowmouse smiled at Beatrice as if she were a very bright witch, indeed. "The region where Bromwich is imprisoned, in the dungeon of his own castle, has remained essentially unchanged. But in each of the other four regions, where Bromwich's four daughters are held captive, one of the basic elements became dominant, resulting in a land of extremes."

"The dominant element in Winter Wood was air," Beatrice said. "That's why it was so cold, and buried under ice and snow."

"Correct!" Dr. Featherstone exclaimed. "And when you reversed Dally Rumpe's spell on Winter Wood, the ice and snow melted, Dally Rumpe melted with it, and Bromwich's daughter Rhona was freed."

"The dominant element in Werewolf Close was earth," Dr. Meadowmouse said. "So it was always hot and dry. When you reversed that part of the spell, the extreme heat and drought went away—as did Dally Rumpe—and Bromwich's second daughter, Innes, was released."

Teddy had been peering over Dr. Meadowmouse's shoulder at *The Bailiwick Family History*. "So now it's time to go to the eastern region," she said.

"That's right," Dr. Featherstone replied. "Sea-Dragon Bay."

"The name tells it all," Dr. Meadowmouse said to Beatrice. "The dominant element is water. Except for some sandbars and rocky islands, the entire region *consists* of water. The bay is filled with every type of deadly sea monster you can imagine. And there are also dangerous rip currents and undertows that could carry a large ship out to sea with no problem and crash it to splinters against the rocks."

"Sea monsters. Rip currents." Beatrice blew her bangs aside and said, "Okay, got it."

Dr. Meadowmouse looked up from the passage he was scanning. "But there's more, Beatrice."

Of course, there's more, Beatrice thought. There were always a zillion impossible things for them to overcome.

"Bromwich's third daughter, Ailsa, is imprisoned on an island in the bay," Dr. Meadowmouse told her. "To reach the island, you must get past the rip currents and undertow, and avoid—uh—"

"Being devoured by sea monsters?" Teddy supplied.

"Er—yes." Dr. Meadowmouse frowned. "Though I would have stated it more delicately."

Teddy shrugged. "No point in beating around the bush," she said.

"There are also cutthroat pirates on the island, as well as scorpions whose sting can kill," Dr. Meadowmouse went on. "And a giant sea serpent guards Ailsa night and day. His name is Hissyfit."

At this, Beatrice felt a knot forming in her stomach. "A serpent," she said, her face looking pinched. "You mean a snake. A giant snake."

Dr. Meadowmouse hesitated, then nodded. "It's a sea creature, but—basically, yes. Ailsa is guarded by a giant water snake."

"I don't know . . ." Beatrice said softly.

Dr. Featherstone placed her hand on Beatrice's arm and said quickly, "But you've fought werewolves—and even a dragon! Surely, Beatrice, a sea serpent is no worse than a dragon."

"I *really* don't like snakes," Beatrice said.

Teddy gave Beatrice a look that said *Don't blow it.* "But we'll manage," Teddy said firmly. "Won't we, Beatrice?"

Beatrice wondered how everyone would react if she just stopped the test right here and now. Teddy would be devastated and probably never speak to her again. Dr. Featherstone would be terribly disappointed, and Dr. Thigpin would assert that he had been right about Beatrice all along. *I knew she didn't have the stuff to be Classical,* he would say. But the worst part—and the only thing that had made her stick with it this far—was knowing that Bromwich and two of his daughters were still Dally Rumpe's prisoners. And likely to remain that way for a very long time unless someone helped them. Crazy or not, this duty seemed to be resting squarely on Beatrice's shoulders. What choice did she have?

"Yes," Beatrice said without conviction. "We'll manage."

Everyone looked relieved.

"The rest is the same as before," Dr. Meadowmouse said to Beatrice. "You must recite the counterspell in Ailsa's presence. Once you've done that, the spell on Sea-Dragon Bay will be broken, Ailsa will be free, and Dally Rumpe will never be able to set foot in the region again."

"I understand," Beatrice said.

"Peregrine, do you have the map?" Dr. Featherstone asked.

Peregrine retrieved a sheet of rolled-up parchment from inside his robes and spread it out on the desk. Beatrice, Teddy, and Mr. and Mrs. Bailey leaned in close to look.

Beatrice had seen this map of Bailiwick before each trip, with details always added for the place they would be visiting. This time, she noticed that a cluster of buildings had been drawn in along the coast. "Is there a village here?" she asked.

"The town of Sea-Dragon Bay," Dr. Meadowmouse replied. "The frequent sightings of sea monsters, as well as the allure of Dally Rumpe's curse and a young captive witch, have always made it a popular beach resort."

"But that's changed now."

At the sound of Dr. Thigpin's voice, they all turned to look at him.

"The number of visitors to Sea-Dragon Bay has dropped off sharply in recent months," the director went on. "And now the town is on the brink of bankruptcy."

"What happened to the tourists?" Beatrice asked.

"Thaddeus." Dr. Featherstone had moved to the director's side. Beatrice could hear the tension in her voice as Aura Featherstone asked, "Does Beatrice really need to know this?"

"She'll find out once she gets there," Dr. Thigpin replied tersely. "I think it's better that she know going in."

Beatrice looked from Dr. Featherstone's troubled face to Dr. Thigpin's unreadable one. *Strange, he isn't even scowling,* Beatrice thought. And that made her nervous.

"So what happened?" Beatrice repeated.

Dr. Thigpin's ice-blue eyes came to rest on her. "*You* happened, Beatrice Bailiwick. Since you started breaking Dally Rumpe's spell, he's more determined than ever to hold on to the regions that remain under his control."

Confused, Beatrice stammered, "But—what does that have to do with tourists staying away?"

"Beatrice." Dr. Thigpin said her name without a hint of impatience. That was surprising enough. Then Beatrice realized that he had never spoken her given name before without adding the Bailiwick. He was being almost *kind!* Now Beatrice was really worried.

"Dally Rumpe is determined to keep Sea-Dragon Bay for himself," Dr. Thigpin said. "He's sending the sea monsters closer and closer to shore, despite the bonfires that are meant to frighten them off, and they're becoming more aggressive by the day. Several witches barely escaped death when they were swimming in what used to be safe areas. So tourists are afraid to come to Sea-Dragon Bay."

"Beatrice isn't to blame for that," Dr. Featherstone said sharply.

Dr. Thigpin looked at Beatrice steadily. "The town is in desperate trouble," he said, "and the residents blame you."

"I see," Beatrice said softly. "I'll be going to a town where everyone hates me."

"No, no," Dr. Meadowmouse protested. "They don't *hate* you. They're just worried and feel the need to blame someone. But, Beatrice, you'll have support in Sea-Dragon Bay. Your family is there."

"The Bailiwicks," Dr. Featherstone added.

Beatrice turned to look at her father.

He shrugged apologetically. "I don't know them, sweetheart."

"Your great-uncle Xenos owns several businesses in town," Dr. Meadowmouse said, "and he's the mayor of Sea-Dragon Bay, as well. There's also his sister, Bridget, your aunt Zara and uncle Ulysses, and three young cousins. All boys, of course, since you're the only Bailiwick female in your generation."

Beatrice was feeling depressed—and a little sorry for herself. "I don't know that having family there is a plus," she said. "Not when they're all suffering because of me."

"Applesauce!" Dr. Thigpin burst out, and the scowl was back. "Hear me clearly, Beatrice Bailiwick," he said, his expression especially fierce. "What you've done is good and right. Sometimes innocent people suffer when we stand up to evil, but we can't turn a blind eye to the likes of Dally Rumpe. Once the witches in Sea-Dragon Bay have had time to think about it, they'll stop blaming you. So toughen up, girl. Nobody ever said that being a witch is easy."

This pronouncement left Beatrice speechless. What she'd done was good and right? And *Dr. Thigpin* was saying this? Then she noticed Dr. Featherstone giving the institute director an approving look.

"Besides," Dr. Meadowmouse jumped in, "when you break the spell on Sea-Dragon Bay, the tourists will come back. Those lovely beaches and the sea are enough to attract visitors. They don't need sea monsters."

If *we can break the spell*, Beatrice thought.

"Beatrice, you and your friends will leave Monday morning," Dr. Featherstone said. "Oh, yes—and a reporter will be going with you."

Beatrice and Teddy's eyes met. Teddy giggled.

"Sasha Leake?" Beatrice asked.

"That's right," Aura Featherstone said. "We could hardly say no and risk offending the media. The Institute could use some positive press for a change. And another young witch will be accompanying you, as well. Miranda Pengilly."

This time, Beatrice and Teddy stared at Dr. Featherstone in alarm.

"The Pengillys are highly respected in the Sphere," Dr. Featherstone continued, without seeming to notice their reactions. "Perhaps you've heard of Miranda's grandfather, Donato Pengilly. He wrote that wonderful book, *The Old Witch and the Sea*."

"But what about Miranda?" Beatrice asked anxiously. "What do you know about her?"

There followed a heavy silence, and Aura Featherstone's eyes appeared strangely veiled. But then the moment passed, and the older witch was saying pleasantly, "Very little, as a matter of fact. Except for her family connections."

"Why are you letting her go with us?" Beatrice persisted.

At this, the calm and cool Dr. Featherstone actually looked flustered. "Approval came from a higher level," she admitted. "I imagine someone in the Institute knows her family. Now, I think we're finished here," she said hastily, "so the committee will leave and let you all get some sleep."

But Beatrice wasn't about to give up without some answers. "How can we find out who gave Miranda permission to go with us?"

"You can't," Dr. Featherstone said flatly. "I've asked. And been told to mind my own business."

4

Mayday!

Beatrice was hauling her bulging backpack down the stairs when Teddy, Ollie, and Cyrus arrived. Mrs. Bailey answered their knock and the three burst into the front hall, all talking at once.

"Ready for the beach, Beatrice?" Cyrus called out.

"Will it be warm enough to swim?" Teddy wondered aloud. "I bought a new bathing suit, just in case."

"I wouldn't recommend swimming," Ollie advised seriously, "until we've done something about those sea monsters."

"Oh," Teddy said. "Good point." Then she added brightly, "Maybe there's a pool."

They drifted out to the porch and Mrs. Bailey started dispensing brown-bag lunches. Mr. Bailey helped Ollie with their backpacks.

The sun was just beginning to brush the tops of the trees when Peregrine suddenly materialized on the front steps. The small witch was wearing his usual dusty brown robes, but Beatrice was surprised to see that he had added some jazzy new accessories. First, there was the chocolate-brown witch's hat, with a band that appeared to be real gold. Beatrice thought it looked very expensive. Then she noticed the watch. Definitely gold, and very heavy. Even Peregrine's shoes were new. His long skinny feet were covered in soft leather slippers that appeared to have been handmade by an expert craftsman.

"Wow, Peregrine," Teddy said, before Beatrice could comment. "Don't you look cool. That hat is really something. And the watch!"

"Yeah," Cyrus chimed in. "Where did you get all the new stuff?"

Everyone was staring at him now. Peregrine turned pink and ducked his head. "They were gifts," he murmured.

"Who from?" Teddy asked.

Peregrine cleared his throat and studied the tops of his sumptuously shod feet. "I don't know," he answered.

Teddy's curiosity was piqued. "What do you mean, you don't know?"

"Don't badger him, Teddy," Beatrice said.

"I'm just asking."

"The gifts—" Peregrine started, then cleared his throat again, "were left on my desk at the Institute." The witch looked up shyly, caught six pairs of eyes on him, and dropped his gaze again. "There was a birthday card with them."

"Was it your birthday?" Ollie asked.

Peregrine shook his head. "Well—no. Not for six more months."

"Was the card signed?" Cyrus wanted to know.

Peregrine's face flushed deep crimson as he nodded.

"So?" Teddy persisted. "Who signed it?"

At this, Peregrine's face flamed until even his ears turned red. Dropping his head still lower, he mumbled something.

"What?" Teddy asked. "I couldn't hear you."

Screwing up his face as if a response required all of his courage, Peregrine said, quite loudly for him, "It was signed 'From your secret admirer.'" Then he looked up, his eyes narrowed and his chin jutting out, as if defying anyone to laugh.

No one did. In truth, Beatrice was touched, and suspected that everyone else was, too. *Imagine that.* Someone had a crush on Peregrine. And why not? He was sweet and thoughtful and really quite adorable!

"That's nice, Peregrine," Beatrice said.

"It is," Teddy agreed.

"Way to go, old man," Ollie said with a gentle grin for Peregrine.

Seeing that they were genuinely pleased for him, Peregrine began to relax and his large ears lost most of their red glow.

"So do you know who it is?" Cyrus asked him.

Now Peregrine appeared deeply perplexed. "I have no idea," he admitted.

"It's someone with plenty of money," Teddy declared. "And she wouldn't have spent so much on you if she planned to stay anonymous. She'll come forward, Peregrine. Trust me."

Peregrine blinked rapidly, his expression changing to one of alarm. "Oh, do you think so?" he asked nervously.

"Don't worry about it," Beatrice said, patting his arm as she gave Teddy a warning look. "You might *never* find out who sent you the gifts."

"That would be fine," Peregrine muttered. "I wouldn't mind at all."

Beatrice was zipping Cayenne into a pocket of her backpack, so that only the cat's head was visible, when she caught sight of Sasha Leake trotting down the street. The witch reporter saw her looking and began to grin and wave.

"Sorry I'm late," Sasha said breathlessly as she bounced up the front walk. She stopped when she saw Peregrine and reached into her pocket for a small black notebook. "Let's see here," Sasha muttered as she flipped through pages. Then she looked up and beamed at the witch adviser. "You must be Peregrine. I'll need to talk to you."

Peregrine was looking mildly alarmed again.

"Peregrine, this is Sasha Leake," Beatrice said. To reassure him, she added, "The committee gave her permission to go with us. She's a reporter."

"And here comes our other traveling companion," Teddy said in a flat voice.

Miranda Pengilly was sidling across the yard toward them. *And taking her own sweet time about it*, Beatrice thought. Today the girl was wearing silky black pants and a black crocheted sweater with glittering onyx beads across the front. Beatrice noticed Teddy eyeing that sweater enviously.

Miranda climbed the steps slowly, steering gracefully around Peregrine and Sasha, until she came to stand beside Beatrice. That had been a deliberate move, Beatrice felt, because Miranda seemed to enjoy the fact that she could now look down at Beatrice. As the girl calmly stared at her, Beatrice realized without a doubt that Miranda Pengilly disliked her. There was no mistaking the animosity in those gray eyes.

Beatrice edged away, and Miranda said coolly, "Shall we go, or are we going to stand around all day?"

"What a witch," Cyrus said under his breath.

Hearing him, Teddy's eyes lit up in delight and she laughed. But she stopped abruptly when Miranda's silver eyes slid ominously toward her.

"Well," Teddy said, turning her back on Miranda and starting down the steps. "I guess we might as well get this show on the road."

There were hugs and kisses from Mr. and Mrs. Bailey, and admonitions to stay safe and not take any unnecessary risks. Mrs. Bailey thrust lunches at Peregrine and Sasha, who bubbled over with gratitude, and at Miranda, who did not. Then they all fell into step behind Peregrine, who had started off down the street.

At the intersection, Peregrine turned right and headed into the woods. Beatrice was following on Peregrine's heels, with Miranda right behind her. Beatrice kept hearing the girl grumble and sputter. "Briars, *yuck!* My clothes will be ruined. Aren't there any paths in this jungle? *Mud.* All over my good shoes!"

Beatrice glanced around and caught sight of Teddy's grinning face. No doubt about it . . . Teddy was enjoying this.

The trees began to thin out and they emerged into a large open field. Their eyes were drawn immediately to the center of the field, where a huge hot-air balloon was anchored. The balloon was bright green with a blue cap on the top. The sight of it took Beatrice's breath away.

There were *oohs* and *ahhs* from the rest of them, and the corners of Peregrine's mouth lifted into a crooked smile. "So you like it?" he asked shyly.

"It's—it's absolutely incredible," Cyrus responded, his eyes huge and round. "We're going to get to ride in it?"

"All the way to the Witches' Sphere," Peregrine said happily.

Beatrice had lowered her backpack to the ground and she noticed that Cayenne's eyes were as round as Cyrus's—but the expression in them was dubious. Beatrice smiled and stooped down to scratch behind the cat's ear. "It's okay," she soothed. "You'll be up there soaring with the birds."

"Oh, this is better than I expected," Sasha said, appearing absolutely thrilled. She reached for her notebook and began to scribble. "Bailey and her companions would be flying first class . . ." Sasha muttered as she wrote.

Beatrice saw that several men were holding on to the wicker basket beneath the balloon. Another man stepped out of the basket and waved to them. He was tall and white haired, with a face turned to leather by the sun.

"Welcome," the man said cordially. "I'm your pilot, Cornelius Wrenn. Are you ready to come aboard?" Then he frowned as his eyes traveled over the group. "But you can't all go. You won't fit."

"Good planning," Miranda muttered, and shot Peregrine a disgusted look.

"No problem," Peregrine said stoutly, cutting his eyes at Miranda. "We have a witch here who can shrink us," he informed the pilot.

"Oh, that should work," Cornelius Wrenn said. "Then have your witch get on with it and we'll take off—while we still have a good east wind."

"Wait a minute," Miranda said, and Beatrice had the pleasure of seeing the girl look less than composed for once. "I don't want to be shrunk. You witches don't have a thimbleful of talent among you. How do I know you can make me normal size again?"

Cyrus drew himself up to his full height and said quietly, "I've *never* had anything go wrong. And I've been doing this since I was five."

"But if you're worried, Miranda," Teddy said sweetly, "you can always decide not to go."

Miranda's eyes slid grimly from Cyrus to Teddy, then came to rest on Beatrice's face. "Not an option," Miranda snapped. And to Cyrus she said, "Do whatever it is you do. And *don't* mess up."

Cyrus told them all to hold hands, and then he chanted the spell. A moment later, they had shrunk to three inches tall. Everyone, that is, except Cornelius Wrenn, who had to remain large to pilot the balloon.

The pilot was now stowing their backpacks on the bench inside the basket. "You can sit on top of these," he said as he lifted Beatrice and Teddy inside. "That way, you'll be able to see out."

Beatrice sat down on her backpack beside Cayenne and looked around. High above her head, a flame shot up into the balloon, filling it with heated air.

"This is *so* neat," Sasha squealed as the pilot lifted her and Miranda to the top of a backpack. "I can't believe it. What a story!"

"Why don't you write it now?" Miranda suggested irritably. "Instead of talking."

"Oh—okay," Sasha said agreeably, and reached into her pocket for her notebook.

Cornelius Wrenn lifted a lever, and suddenly the flame over their heads shot higher.

"Okay, we're about ready to go," he told them.

The pilot motioned to the men who held the basket, and they stepped back. The balloon rocked gently for a moment. Then it began to rise.

Beatrice held her breath, expecting to be scared. But as the balloon rose steadily upward, she began to relax and enjoy it. She felt as if she were sailing through the sky on a cloud. The wind blew gently through her hair and the sun bathed her face in warmth. It was lovely!

When Beatrice looked down, she was surprised at how quickly they had left Earth behind. Woods and fields were far below them now, and the houses looked no bigger than the plastic ones on a Monopoly board.

Cyrus's expression was ecstatic as he leaned over the edge of the basket. Then he turned to Cornelius Wrenn and said, "How do you steer this thing, anyway?"

"You don't," the pilot replied. "Wind moves in different directions at different altitudes, so if you want to change directions, you move the balloon higher or lower. Then you just ride the winds."

"It doesn't sound very precise," Ollie said thoughtfully.

"Not very," the pilot agreed without apparent concern. "But it usually works."

Miranda twisted around to look at him. "*Usually?*"

After a while, the sunlight began to dim, as if a giant gray cloud had moved in to cover them. Beatrice noticed that her companions' faces were becoming indistinct, and they were soon lost in darkness. Beatrice knew this meant that they were entering The Borderlands, the region that lay between the mortal world and the Witches' Sphere.

An unexpected gust of wind caused the basket to lurch, then rock violently. The movement made Beatrice feel queasy. Close by, she heard a moan.

"Teddy?" Beatrice said. "Are you all right?"

"I'm fine," came Teddy's voice from the darkness.

"Well, I'm not."

It was Miranda speaking, and she sounded shaky.

Beatrice moved in the direction of the girl's voice, reaching out until she touched Miranda's arm. The girl jerked away from Beatrice's hand.

"Try breathing deeply," Beatrice said, and decided to take her own advice as the basket started rocking again.

Another moan, and then Miranda said weakly, "I don't need your help. I can take care of myself."

Beatrice's sympathy for the girl faded. Miranda Pengilly really was a nasty person, no matter *who* she was.

The balloon was moving smoothly again, and Beatrice felt better. Then she noticed the darkness was starting to lift.

"We're entering the Witches' Sphere," Peregrine said, and immediately Beatrice began to worry.

She had tried not to think too much about Sea-Dragon Bay and what would be waiting for her there. But now that their arrival was imminent, Beatrice was forced to admit that she was apprehensive. *Sea monsters and giant serpents are enough to make anyone jittery,* she told herself—without the added burden of being resented by a whole town! *That's* what had Beatrice most worried. What if her own family hated her? And, even worse, what if she failed them?

The sky had turned from gray to a brilliant cloudless blue. Beatrice surfaced from her brooding and peered down. The view that met her eyes was astonishingly beautiful!

It was a land of golden sand stretching as far as she could see, with green grasses dancing atop the dunes and a strip of turquoise water on the horizon. The colors were so vibrant, and the sun's reflection on the sand so intense, the effect was dazzling.

The balloon sailed on, drawing closer to the sea. At the edge of the water, Beatrice could see a street winding along the coastline with buildings on either side. Sitting off by itself was a large turreted structure that looked like a giant sand castle. And beyond the castle, on a sandbar that was nearly surrounded by water, rose a tall black tower. The tower stood out starkly—dark and forbidding—in the sun-drenched landscape. Beatrice felt drawn to the tower and couldn't take her eyes off it. But then the flames caught her attention.

For a moment, Beatrice thought the water was on fire. But then she realized that a string of tiny islands ran parallel to the shoreline, and a huge bonfire burned on each of the islands.

Peregrine crawled over to sit beside Beatrice. "Welcome to Sea-Dragon Bay," he said.

"It's beautiful," she replied. "Those fires are meant to frighten off the sea monsters?"

"That's right." Peregrine studied the flames for a while, then suddenly pointed to one of them. "Do you see how the fire is taking on a shape? Look closely. There's a head, and a snout, and an eye—"

"It's a dragon!" Beatrice exclaimed. "It looks *exactly* like a dragon."

Peregrine nodded. "Sometimes, when magical fires are meant to be guardians, as these are, they take on the form of a dragon—or *drakes*, as witches refer to them. So we call these guardian bonfires firedrakes."

Beatrice was going to ask about the sand castle when she noticed that they seemed awfully close to the ground. She turned to the pilot.

"Uh—Mr. Wrenn—are we losing altitude?"

"Yes," the pilot answered, "but I'm doing it on purpose. See this cord? I've pulled it to release some of the hot air so that we can begin to descend. I'm going to land on that broad stretch of sand just south of town."

"That's pretty close to the water," Ollie said. "Are you sure it's safe?"

"Absolutely," the pilot replied. "This balloon is the very best they make, and it's just had its regular maintenance. Sound as a gold tooth. Now, I'll release the cord," he said, "to slow our descent."

Beatrice saw Cornelius Wrenn's hand relax on the cord. Almost instantly, she noticed a strange look come over his face. He pulled on the cord and released it again. Pull, release. Pull, release. Beatrice didn't know anything about balloons, but she didn't think the pilot's jerky movements seemed right.

"Mr. Wrenn," Beatrice asked, "is something wrong?"

The pilot was still pulling and releasing the cord—frantically, it seemed to Beatrice. She was pretty sure they were in trouble.

The balloon was still losing altitude, and instead of following the coast to the spot where Cornelius Wrenn had intended to land, it was drifting out over the water.

The pilot reached for the radio. "*Mayday, Mayday,*" he said into the receiver. "Balloon going down over Sea-Dragon Bay. *Mayday!*"

All the passengers had leaped to their feet.

"This can't be happening," Teddy said softly.

Beatrice reached for Teddy's hand. With her other hand, she unzipped Cayenne's pocket and stroked the cat. "We're going to be fine," she whispered. "Don't be scared, Cay."

The balloon was sinking closer and closer to the water. Cornelius Wrenn dropped the radio receiver and turned to Cyrus. "Make them big again," the pilot ordered. "Even if I can manage to land on this side of the bonfires, you'll never make it to shore as small as you are. *Do it. Now!*"

No one asked any questions. They all scrambled over to Cyrus and he cast the spell to return them to normal size. While Cyrus chanted, Beatrice thought, *Swim to shore . . . sea monsters in the water . . . rip currents . . .*

Just as Beatrice realized that she was her normal size again, and was grabbing for Cayenne, the basket hit the water. Hard! Pain shot up Beatrice's leg and spine. She heard screaming, and then she was thrown from the basket, still clutching Cayenne to her chest.

In Beatrice's last conscious moment, she plunged into ice-cold water. Beatrice whispered, "Swim, Cayenne. Swim." Then a rip current seized her and pulled her under.

5

The Ghost Guard

*B*eatrice came to with a start. Cold water was churning around her, sloshing into her eyes and her ears, and threatening to pull her under again. Instinctively, Beatrice began to kick to stay afloat.

Then she heard a voice in her ear saying, "Don't fight it. I've got you."

It was Ollie's voice, and Ollie's arm around her, holding her head above the water.

In that confused moment, Beatrice felt relief—Ollie had saved her, Ollie was alive—and then panic when she realized that Cayenne was no longer in her arms.

"Cayenne!" Beatrice thought she was shouting, but she could barely hear the strangled sound of her own voice. She took a deep breath before calling out again, but her lungs didn't seem to be working. A burning pain spread through her chest as she gasped for air.

Beatrice was whimpering now, certain that Cayenne had been lost beneath the waves. But Ollie was saying, "Look, Beatrice. She's here."

Beatrice turned her head toward him and saw Cayenne pressed against his shoulder, hanging on for dear life.

Beatrice's body went limp and she started to cry. *Everything's going to be all right*, she thought. But then she remembered: There were sea monsters in these waters.

Beatrice jerked her head around, trying to get her bearings. The firedrakes were behind her, their flames rising into the sky from the dark blue-green water. And ahead was the shoreline—but it looked very far away. Beatrice told herself they could make it to shore, but she didn't believe it. Her arms and legs were numb from the cold water. How could they ever swim that far, especially with the undertow and rip currents?

A door slammed shut in Beatrice's mind. She wouldn't think about that now. What she needed to do was find her friends.

The balloon was spread out flat across the water at the base of one of the firedrake islands, the green nylon billowing a little as the wind grabbed and lifted it.

"Do you see anyone else?" Beatrice asked Ollie. Her voice was raspy and her chest still burned. It was difficult to speak.

"Over there." Ollie pointed.

Beatrice's eyes searched the choppy waters around the balloon. Then she saw them—two tiny figures holding on to yellow flotation cushions. Beatrice squinted against the sun's reflection on the water, and finally she was able to make out their faces. It was Teddy and Peregrine! And floating among the ropes of the balloon was Cornelius Wrenn. But where were the others?

"I don't see Cyrus." A small wave hit Beatrice in the face. She coughed and sputtered. "Or Sasha and Miranda—"

"There," Ollie said, and pointed again.

Sure enough, three heads bobbed in the water behind Cornelius.

Beatrice felt another surge of relief. She was wondering if she and Ollie and Cayenne would be able to reach the others—and if they could, how they'd all manage to make it to shore—when she suddenly became aware of a distant roar. Beatrice's heart leaped. It sounded like a plane!

She threw back her head and scanned the sky. But all she saw were some gulls flying overhead.

Beatrice felt sick with disappointment. She held on tighter to Ollie and placed a protective arm around Cayenne. The cat let out a plaintive cry. *How much longer can we stay afloat?* Beatrice wondered. There didn't seem to be any way out of this.

But she could still hear the sound of a motor. And it seemed closer now. Beatrice lifted her face from Ollie's shoulder, and she saw a large white boat emerging from between two of the firedrakes. And it was heading for them!

"Ollie!" Beatrice's voice came out strong this time. She was bouncing in his arms and pointing. "Look, Ollie—a boat!"

Ollie's face broke into a grin. Then he laughed out loud. They were both laughing and shouting and waving frantically. Beatrice saw that the others were doing the same.

The boat stopped near the balloon. Figures in dark blue uniforms were moving swiftly across the deck. Ropes were being thrown to Cornelius Wrenn and the others.

Beatrice watched as, one by one, their fellow travelers were towed in and taken aboard the boat. Then the craft's motor started again and it moved toward Beatrice, Ollie, and Cayenne.

A flotation ring on the end of a rope landed near Beatrice. After Ollie put the ring over her head and secured it under her arms, Beatrice pried Cayenne's claws loose from Ollie's jacket and pulled the cat to her. Beatrice's teeth were chattering now. She was too weary and numb to even think, but she was vaguely aware of being pulled through the water toward the boat. She twisted around anxiously to look for Ollie and then relaxed when she saw that he was being towed in after her.

Beatrice felt herself being lifted from the water and then lowered to the deck of the boat. But her legs felt rubbery and wouldn't support her. She sank to the floor in relief and buried her face against Cayenne's wet fur.

When Beatrice heard someone calling her name, she looked up—and found herself staring into the wispy, transparent faces of a half-dozen ghosts.

Beatrice blinked. She wondered if she was hallucinating. But, no, there they were: a circle of ghosts wearing dark blue uniforms and peering down at her with kindly concern. They had embroidered patches on their shirts that read: *Ghost Guard*.

Teddy and Cyrus came to the edge of the circle, wrapped in blankets and appearing nearly as pale as the ghosts. Beatrice had never been so happy to see them.

"Are you all right?" she asked. "Is Peregrine—?"

"We're fine," Teddy said, her voice no more than a thin whisper. "Everyone's fine. It was you and Ollie we were worried about."

"Well, I'm fine, too." A bedraggled Ollie came and sat down beside Beatrice. He draped a blanket around her and Cayenne.

Then Peregrine rushed over—minus his new hat, Beatrice noticed, his ears looking especially large with his hair plastered flat—followed by Cornelius Wrenn, Sasha, and Miranda.

"Blesséd be," Peregrine said anxiously. "Is anyone hurt? This is *all* my fault." He started wringing his hands, looking like he might burst into tears. "I never should have brought you in that balloon. Your parents *trusted* me! It's all my fault."

"It wasn't the balloon." Cornelius Wrenn had stepped forward and was frowning down at Peregrine. "I tested that cord yesterday and it was working fine. It's almost brand new, in fact. There was nothing wrong with the cord."

"But I saw you jerking on it, and it didn't work," Ollie said. "So what happened?"

Cornelius Wrenn's face darkened. "Magic," he said grimly. "Someone cast a spell on it."

Beatrice and Ollie exchanged a look.

"I'm certain of it," the pilot insisted. "I've worked with balloons all my life and I've never seen this happen before. It was magic. I'd stake my life on it."

Teddy sat down close to Beatrice. "Dally Rumpe?" she whispered.

Beatrice shrugged, not knowing what to think. After all, accidents *did* happen. Then her eyes slid to Miranda Pengilly. Except for being wet, it was difficult to believe the girl had just experienced a balloon crash. Everyone else appeared dazed and anxious, but Miranda was perfectly composed. Beatrice couldn't be sure, but she thought she even detected a glint of amusement in the girl's gray eyes. Or was it *satisfaction?*

After two mugs of hot witch's brew, Beatrice and her companions felt better. So much better that Teddy said suddenly, "I just realized—all our clothes are at the bottom of the bay."

Cyrus gave her a sidelong glance. "You can't tell me that you're worried about *clothes*, Teddy. We're lucky to be alive!"

"Oh, I know," Teddy said impatiently. "But I bought new stuff for the trip, and now no one will even see it."

"*I* had some designer originals in my bag," Miranda informed them.

Sasha smiled ruefully. "All I had was junk."

Then Beatrice noticed Peregrine's bare head, and said, "You've lost your new hat."

"And my watch," the witch adviser replied. "But they can be replaced."

Teddy wasn't so philosophical. "Think how we'll look when we go ashore," she said. "I don't even have a hair dryer now."

Beatrice sighed. She loved Teddy—really, she did—but sometimes her friend's vanity was more than she could comprehend. "No one expects you to look like a super-model after you've just crashed into the sea," Beatrice assured her. "And we can buy new clothes—and new *hair dryers*—in town. So chill out, Teddy."

The air temperature, unlike the water, was warm. Beatrice realized that her hair and clothes were nearly dry by the time the Ghost Guard boat pulled up to the pier.

"I wonder why we didn't have a problem with rip currents," Beatrice said as they prepared to go ashore.

"Because we're in a ghost boat," Cornelius Wrenn answered, "and since it isn't composed of matter, natural phenomena can't have any effect on it."

This gave Beatrice an idea. "Then maybe the Ghost Guard could help us reach Ailsa's island," she said.

Peregrine shook his head. "That's against regulation. Civilians aren't allowed on Ghost Guard boats—unless they're being rescued, of course."

Before leaving the boat, Beatrice shook each ghost's hand—which was a bizarre experience, since she couldn't actually *feel* their hands—and thanked them before walking down the ramp to dry land. Everyone else expressed their appreciation, as well, except for Miranda. *She* was complaining because the Ghost Guard refused to send down a diver to bring up her bag.

The first thing Beatrice noticed as they walked down the pier toward town was that everything looked as golden and sparkling on the ground as it had from the air. Most of the shops and houses were made of sandstone that blended in with the landscape, relying on a brightly painted door or colorful flowers to set them apart from the dunes.

The second thing Beatrice noticed was that there didn't appear to be any people here. The narrow cobbled street that ran through the center of town was deserted, and even the shops appeared to be empty. Beatrice pondered this as they passed one darkened window after another. Was the financial situation in Sea-Dragon Bay so desperate that all the residents had been forced to leave?

"Where is everybody?" Cyrus asked.

"It's certainly strange," Sasha said, and reached for her notebook. "Boy! First a crash landing and now a ghost town."

"This is very odd," Peregrine murmured. "I would have expected to see people at the pier watching the rescue."

"They're busy. Elsewhere," came a voice from behind them.

Beatrice and her companions spun around, startled by a break in the silence that hung over the town. Standing there was a gangly, long-boned man with a shock of dark hair that needed combing and eyes like deep black holes in a colorless face. He rubbed his palms nervously down the sides of his faded olive-green robes and blinked several times.

"Busy with what?" Peregrine asked.

"Town meeting," the man replied. He blinked again, fidgeting a little as he peered at each of them in turn. "Oh. Forgive me. For not introducing myself." He scratched at the stubble on his chin. "I'm Wadsworth Fretwell. At your service. And I know who you are," he said, turning his gaze on Beatrice. "I've seen your picture in the paper. Lots of times." He folded his long arms across his chest, seemed uncomfortable with that, and unfolded them again. "You're Beatrice Bailiwick. And you probably want to see your great-uncle Xenos. But you can't."

This guy is plenty strange, Beatrice thought. "I can't?" she asked.

"He's the mayor," Wadsworth replied. "So he's at the meeting. Running it, actually. So, no. You can't see him."

"What's the meeting about?" Teddy asked.

Wadsworth's eyes darted warily from Teddy to Beatrice. "Well—it's about saving the town. A lot of businesses have shut down. The rest may close soon." He looked solemnly at Beatrice. "Everyone's mad at you," he said. "Except me. I'm not mad."

"And why is that?" Ollie asked. "Why is everyone mad except you?"

Wadsworth shrugged, then smiled, seemed to think better of it, and put on a serious face again. "Well—she didn't really *mean* to destroy our town, did she?" he asked reasonably. "It wasn't *deliberate*. And I try not to judge."

Beatrice didn't know how to respond to this, so she said, "I think *we* should go to the meeting."

Peregrine gave her a worried look, as did Wadsworth Fretwell.

"I don't know about that," Peregrine said.

"I'm not sure it's wise," Wadsworth said, scratching at his neck. "You'll only get your feelings hurt."

"I'm going," Beatrice said stiffly, "but it's kind of you to be concerned."

"I try to have compassion," Wadsworth said.

"Where is this meeting?" Ollie asked.

"City Hall," Wadsworth said. "I'll take you there. If you're quite certain," he added to Beatrice.

"*Quite* certain," Beatrice answered.

They said their good-byes to Cornelius Wrenn, expressing their thanks and their sympathy over the loss of his balloon.

"I'm insured," he said. Then he shook his head, looking troubled. "Just take special care," he advised Beatrice as he turned to leave them. "This *wasn't* an accident."

Wadsworth Fretwell started down the street, and the others fell into step behind him. Between stumbling over cobbles and bumping into street signs, Wadsworth pointed out features of interest.

"The Firedrake Inn," Wadsworth said as they approached a sprawling gray clapboard building overlooking the bay. "Owned by Xenos Bailiwick. The Sea Witch Gallery," he said, of the smaller gray building next door. "Owned by Xenos Bailiwick."

After they had passed a dozen businesses, at least half of which were owned by Beatrice's great-uncle, Ollie grinned at Beatrice. "I wonder why they don't just name the town Bailiwick."

"That's being discussed," Wadsworth said, craning his long neck around to look at them, and promptly tripping over a curb. "At the meeting."

He stopped in front of an official-looking building with a sign that read *City Hall*. "So. Here we are."

But Beatrice's attention was directed farther down the street. Sitting off to itself was the sand castle she had seen from the air. It was very large and built of gold-colored sandstone. There were round turrets at each corner and a massive arch that led into a courtyard.

Ollie came to stand with Beatrice. "Wow," he said. "I wonder what kid made that."

Beatrice smiled. "So you think it looks like a sand castle, too."

"That's why it's *called* The Sandcastle," Wadsworth said. "And it's owned by—"

"Xenos Bailiwick," Beatrice and Ollie finished together.

"Exactly," Wadsworth said, and scratched his ear.

6

A Grim Welcome

Wadsworth Fretwell led them inside and down a long hall. As they approached a door at the end, Beatrice could hear the sounds of muffled voices on the other side. But then Wadsworth opened the door a crack and she got the full force of several raised voices, all determined to be heard over the others.

Wadsworth rubbed his palms together nervously and glanced at Beatrice. "Doesn't sound good. Do you still want to go in?"

No would have been the honest answer, but Beatrice nodded and said, "Yes, I do."

She took a quick steadying breath and walked inside. The room was crowded, with almost every chair filled except for a few empty seats in the back row. Wadsworth motioned Beatrice toward them, and the others followed.

Several people glanced up casually as Beatrice and her companions sat down—and then did a double take. Beatrice was acutely aware of the sudden change in their attitudes as they stared at her, their faces turning to stone. Beatrice figured they must have seen her picture in the paper.

It was really hard to ignore the glowering expressions, not to mention the whispering that had started along the row. Beatrice settled Cayenne into her lap and then looked straight ahead, to the front of the room where a man was standing behind a podium.

He was a small, distinguished-looking witch in gray business robes, with close-cropped salt-and-pepper hair and penetrating dark eyes. Beatrice smiled. Her father's eyes. This had to be Xenos Bailiwick, her great-uncle.

"Now, Argus, let Tolley finish," Xenos was saying calmly. "You'll have your turn."

A stout young man in blue robes was standing near the front and glaring across the room. "As I was *saying*, we need to do something *now*. No one's come in to rent a boat from me in three months. But I don't see the point in changing the town's name. A new name won't make the sea monsters go away."

"Tolley's right," someone called from the back. "No matter what we call it, everybody in the Sphere will still know it's Sea-Dragon Bay."

Then a middle-aged woman stood up and said, "Xenos, this is *your* fault, you know. I think you should buy us all out!"

"Now, Prudence," another man said. "How do you figure this is Xenos's fault?"

"It was a Bailiwick that got Dally Rumpe all stirred up, wasn't it?" Prudence demanded. "That little troublemaker Beatrice Bailiwick? Xenos, she's *your* niece or whatever. You should have stopped her!"

Beatrice felt her face growing warm, and she wanted to disappear on the spot. Ollie, Cyrus, and Teddy were giving her sympathetic looks, and Sasha was patting Beatrice's arm with one hand while scribbling away with the other. Beatrice couldn't help but cut her eyes around at Miranda, and saw exactly what she had expected. Miranda was smiling. *Gloating.* Beatrice's face turned redder still, but this time it was from anger.

The debate continued, with most people agreeing that their troubles had started when Beatrice Bailiwick came on the scene.

Xenos gave them all a turn, and then he said, "May I speak now?"

There was something about the way he said it that caused the others to quiet down. Maybe because he was the only one not yelling. By contrast, he sounded reasonable and in control.

"Well, Xenos, tell us what's on your mind," Prudence said, still sounding upset, but at a lower volume.

"We all have a lot to lose," Xenos said. "My family has lived in Sea-Dragon Bay for generations—since before it *was* Sea-Dragon Bay. We're just like the rest of you—hurting. The Firedrake Inn hasn't had any overnight guests in months, no one's coming to the gallery, and all our cottages are vacant." Xenos paused and looked out over the crowd. "But we can't blame Beatrice for this."

At that point, people started to mutter and a few shouted out their disagreement.

"Now, hold on," Xenos said, spreading his hands wide. "You think I'm defending Beatrice because she's family—but you're *wrong!* I'm defending her because she's done the right thing."

There was more grumbling from the audience, but Beatrice didn't hear it. She was staring at Xenos, at this soft-spoken man whose face was strained with worry and whose shoulders sagged under the burden he carried. And despite all that, he was taking up for her. Beatrice was so touched—not to mention *relieved* that at least one of the Bailiwicks didn't hate her—she wanted to run up there this minute and throw her arms around Uncle Xenos.

"Think about it," Xenos was saying. "If you condemn someone for trying to end Dally Rumpe's treachery, you're condoning the misery he's caused. You're *helping* him. Is that what you want?"

No one spoke for a moment, then Xenos said, "Of course not. You're good witches, and I know it's hard for you right now. But we need to place the blame where it belongs—and that's at Dally Rumpe's feet, not Beatrice's."

Suddenly Prudence stood up again, scowling at him. "That's all well and good, Xenos, but how are you going to feel when Beatrice Bailiwick shows up *here*? What with Bridget and all. How's your sister going to take it having that hotshot little witch rubbing it in?"

Beatrice saw a subtle change in her great-uncle's face. A spark in his dark eyes. A tightening of his lips. And there was tension in his voice that hadn't been there before when he said quietly, "Leave Bridget out of this, Prudence."

About that time, a man in the front row leaped up and ran to Xenos's side. He had tiny close-set eyes and straw-colored hair that stood out in thin wisps around a pinched face.

"How dare you attack Xenos Bailiwick!" the man cried out. "After all he's done for this town!"

Wadsworth Fretwell leaned down and whispered to Beatrice, "That's Angel Crump. He works for Xenos."

Xenos was patting Angel gently on the back. "It's all right, no need to get upset." And to the room in general, he said, "I think it's time to adjourn this meeting. Everybody, think about what we discussed today, and we'll meet next week to vote on a plan."

There was still a lot of heated conversation as people filed out of the room. Beatrice slumped down with her face lowered until most of the town witches had left.

Miranda had been watching her. "You could have stood up and defended yourself," the girl said to Beatrice. Then she added casually, "Of course, *that* would have taken courage."

"You know something, Miranda?" Teddy said suddenly, her eyes blazing. "I'm getting pretty fed up with you, *whoever* you are. And you don't have any right to talk to Beatrice about courage. She's faced more danger than a hundred other witches put together—and she doesn't even *care* about being a Classical witch. All she wants is to help Bromwich and his daughters."

"I'm glad to hear it," came a man's voice from behind them.

A startled Beatrice turned around to find Xenos Bailiwick standing there. He looked at Beatrice steadily, assessing her. Then he said, "I'm happy to finally meet you, Beatrice," and held out his arms.

After they hugged, Beatrice started to introduce him to everyone, but had only gotten as far as Peregrine when a man and woman walked up. The man looked just like Xenos except that he was younger and his dark hair hadn't started to turn gray.

"Beatrice, this is my son, Ulysses," Xenos said.

Ulysses shook her hand, but there was nothing especially friendly in his expression. In fact, Beatrice had the distinct impression that he wasn't pleased to see her at all.

"So you've come to try and break Dally Rumpe's spell on Sea-Dragon Bay?" Ulysses asked. Without waiting for a reply, he added, "Just so you'll understand, most of us don't *want* the sea monsters to go away."

"Ulysses," Xenos said, his tone a quiet warning.

"What we *want*," Ulysses continued, "is to keep them beyond the firedrakes where they won't do any harm. That's worked well for us all these years."

"Beatrice," Xenos said, drawing her gently away from his son, "I want you to meet Ulysses' wife, Zara."

The woman was also dark. She had a lively, intelligent face and black unruly hair that tumbled past her shoulders. She was wearing burgundy robes and a heavy silver pendent set with garnets.

Xenos regarded Zara with affection. "My favorite daughter-in-law," he said.

"Also, your *only* daughter-in-law," Zara responded, her dark eyes twinkling. Then she turned her full attention to Beatrice. "Oh, my . . . you're gorgeous, aren't you? Just look at that stunning red hair."

No one had ever called Beatrice gorgeous before, or even pretty. She was embarrassed. And pleased.

"Those hooligans over there are my sons," Zara added, her face lighting up as only a doting mother's can.

Beatrice looked across the room to where two little boys were hiding behind a table, waiting for an older boy to find them. All three had their mother's black untamed hair.

"Quincy is the oldest," Zara said. "He's fourteen. And the little ones are Rex and George. They're six and four. Oops! There goes George into the heating vent."

While Zara went running after her sons, Beatrice noticed that Teddy was watching the boys with an intense expression on her face. Beatrice knew that look.

"Quincy?" Beatrice whispered into Teddy's ear.

"He's so cute," Teddy whispered back. "And what a smile."

"Well, you're about to have your chance to charm him," Beatrice said, grinning.

Zara was coming back holding one little boy's hand while the smaller one rode on Quincy's shoulders.

"I want you to meet your cousin, Beatrice, and her friends," Zara was saying.

"I've heard a lot about *you*, Cousin Beatrice," Quincy said, his tone playful and his eyes sparkling with devilment. "But I won't hold it against you."

Beatrice laughed. She liked this cousin.

Beatrice began to introduce her companions, taking note of the way Quincy's eyes lingered on Teddy. *Well, that's working out well*, Beatrice thought.

Then she came to Miranda, who had been oddly reticent and standing off to the side.

"Miranda," Beatrice said to the girl's back.

Miranda Pengilly turned around slowly, and Beatrice saw Quincy's face change. He looked surprised—no, *shocked!*

"What are *you* doing here?" Quincy demanded.

Beatrice's eyes darted from Quincy to Miranda and back again. "You know her?" Beatrice asked, her heart beginning to thump hard in her chest.

But just then Beatrice saw a woman come striding into the room. Beatrice recognized the stern-faced witch from the Witches' Executive Committee.

"Why, that's Eustacia Jones," Peregrine said. "I wonder what she's doing here."

The witch stopped directly in front of Peregrine, but her announcement was for everyone in the room.

"I am Dr. Eustacia Jones, Director of Witch Ethics at the Witches' Institute," she said, as if this were probably the most important job in the world. Then her gum-colored eyes shifted down to Peregrine and her expression grew even more stern. "I am here to inform you, Peregrine, that you are suspended from your position, effective immediately. All duties and privileges connected with that position cease as of this moment."

Peregrine didn't move. He just stared up at the woman as if she had said something too incredible to be believed.

Beatrice was nearly that shocked herself. She hurried over to Peregrine and said, "Dr. Jones, why in the world would Peregrine be suspended? He's the most conscientious witch I know. He cares about his job. He cares about *us*," she added, and saw Ollie and Teddy nodding. "And we *are* his job."

"Not anymore," Dr. Jones said curtly. "And perhaps never again."

Beatrice was beginning to understand that this was really serious. But what could Peregrine have possibly done?

Still appearing stunned, Peregrine roused himself enough to ask, "What is it you think I did?"

"*I* don't think anything," the woman replied. "I'm just carrying out my duties and waiting for the results of the investigation."

Now Peregrine looked terrified. His legs began to tremble and one eye started to twitch. "I'm going to be— *investigated?*" he asked in a quivering voice.

"You are," Dr. Jones said with one decisive nod of her head. "A grave accusation has been made against you."

Beatrice reached out to steady Peregrine. She could feel his whole body shaking under her hand. "But what has he been accused of?" Beatrice cried.

Eustacia Jones looked down at some papers she was holding. "There are several charges," the witch replied, "but all of them basically amount to the same thing. He's been accused of working with Dally Rumpe."

"*No, no,*" Beatrice said quickly. She couldn't have heard that correctly.

Dr. Jones began to read off the charges mechanically. "Providing information to Dally Rumpe . . . Accepting payment from Dally Rumpe . . . Informing Dally Rumpe of Beatrice Bailiwick's scheduled return to the Witches' Sphere . . ."

"*What?!*" Beatrice's head was spinning. The whole *world* seemed to be spinning out of control. "This is a nightmare," Beatrice said softly.

7

Sand Castle with a View

Peregrine was tugging on Beatrice's arm and Beatrice looked down at him.

"I didn't do it," Peregrine said miserably.

"I know you didn't," Beatrice said, equally miserable.

Dr. Jones was stuffing papers into her briefcase. "You aren't allowed to leave Sea-Dragon Bay until the investigation has been completed," she said to Peregrine.

"But I have work back at the Institute—"

Eustacia Jones gave him a hard look. "And naturally, you won't be allowed inside the Institute. You'll have to stay here and wait for the outcome."

Xenos Bailiwick looked sympathetically at Beatrice. "Your friend is welcome to stay with us," he said kindly. "We want you all to stay."

Beatrice smiled gratefully at him. "Thank you, Uncle Xenos," she said. "I'm sure this will be cleared up soon."

"Of course it will!"

Beatrice recognized Aura Featherstone's voice at once, and turning to the door, saw the auburn-haired witch walking quickly toward them. Dr. Meadowmouse was close behind her. One look at their faces and Beatrice knew that they were as horrified—and outraged—as she was.

"Eustacia." Dr. Featherstone nodded curtly to her colleague.

"Aura." Dr. Jones nodded curtly back.

"There's been a mistake," Dr. Featherstone said, her voice deceptively calm. "I've worked with Peregrine ever since I came to the Institute, and he's the most loyal witch I know."

"And he would *never* betray Beatrice," Dr. Meadowmouse added passionately.

Dr. Jones snapped her briefcase shut. "If that's true," she said, all cool efficiency, "then he has nothing to worry about. An investigator will be here to question him—" now her eyes moved over the faces around her, "—and everyone who knows him. Good day, Aura. Leopold."

Beatrice watched the woman march toward the door. *She's just doing her job*, Beatrice told herself. But she could have been nicer. Beatrice knew that she was never going to like Eustacia Jones.

Meanwhile, Dr. Featherstone was talking quietly with Peregrine. Beatrice heard her say, "It's a lot of hogwash! I'm going to find out who filed these charges."

"That's usually kept confidential," Dr. Meadowmouse reminded her. "Unless there's a—" Dr. Meadowmouse stopped and looked unhappily at his feet.

"A trial," Peregrine finished softly. "I could be banished from the Sphere for this."

"That isn't going to happen," Dr. Featherstone said, her hazel eyes blazing. "Try not to worry, Peregrine. We're going to get you out of this."

It was a somber party that left City Hall and started down the street toward The Sandcastle. Beatrice's mind was working overtime as she tried to figure out what was going on. *It has to be Dally Rumpe*, she decided. This would be a clever way to distract Beatrice and her friends and even discourage them enough to make them go home. But Beatrice wasn't going anywhere. She was staying here, no matter what, to help her friend.

She glanced at Peregrine, who was trudging along beside her. His chin was tucked down into the front of his robes, and he looked about as depressed as anyone could.

Quincy fell into step between Beatrice and Teddy.

"You really trust this guy?" Quincy asked quietly, so that Peregrine wouldn't hear.

"Absolutely," Beatrice said.

"No question about it," Teddy agreed.

From Beatrice's shoulder, Cayenne emitted an emphatic *meow*.

Quincy smiled and reached up to scratch behind Cayenne's ear. "Then so do I," Quincy said. "Maybe I can help you figure this out."

Teddy beamed at him.

Sasha squeezed in beside Beatrice. "And I'll help, too," she said.

Beatrice must have looked doubtful because Sasha rushed on. "I know what you're thinking: I'm just a reporter out for a story. And that's true," she admitted.

"But I really like you guys—and no matter *what* my boss thinks, I'm a pretty good investigator. Maybe I can find out who made the accusations against Peregrine."

Beatrice looked into the reporter's earnest face and was touched. "Thanks, Sasha," she said. "We can use all the help we can get."

Then Beatrice remembered Miranda and was tempted to ask Quincy who she was, but Peregrine was sniffling now and they were all so upset, it didn't seem like the right time.

They arrived at The Sandcastle and passed under the towering arch that led into the courtyard. Inside was a tangle of fig and orange trees, palmettos, and flowering vines.

Beatrice and her friends followed Uncle Xenos and the rest of the Bailiwicks through wide double doors into the castle itself. The walls and floors inside were the same golden sandstone, but polished so that they glowed in the sunlight. The ceilings were very high, painted blue like the sky with soft swirling clouds. Crystal chandeliers lined the huge entry hall, sparkling and swaying in the breeze from the sea. But what Beatrice found most amazing were the birds.

Decorative golden cages hung from the walls and the ceiling. There were dozens of them. And inside the cages were large birds with colorful plumage, each appearing more beautiful and exotic than the last.

Beatrice glanced into vast rooms off each side of the hall, and along with overstuffed sofas and polished wood tables, she saw more birds. There were even cages sitting on top of a grand piano.

But then Beatrice noticed the open doors at the far end of the hall and her attention was captured by the breathtaking view of the bay. The sight of the blue-green water caused her to flinch as she remembered how recently she had thought herself lost in those waves.

Beatrice moved toward the open doors, and the tall black tower she had seen from the air came into view. Xenos walked over to stand beside her.

"What is that tower?" Beatrice asked.

"That," Xenos answered softly, "is where my sister, Bridget, lives."

Beatrice heard sadness in his voice, a haunted quality that made her glance at him quickly. She hoped he would say more.

But Xenos only shook his head, as if to clear it of unwelcome thoughts, and then he turned to the others and smiled. "We're happy to have you all here," he said, with such warmth and calm that Beatrice thought she might have imagined his sadness. "We want you to make yourselves at home, and if there's anything you need, please tell us."

"I'm sure you'd all like to wash up and rest awhile before dinner," Zara was saying. Then she stopped as a small figure came dashing down the wide circular staircase.

"Oh, there you are, Kolliwobbles," Zara said. "Will you take Rex and George up for their naps? They can have a glass of dragon's milk first—but *no sweets*."

Kolliwobbles was no more than three feet tall, with skinny legs that bowed out under his blue shorts and even skinnier wrists protruding from the sleeves of his shirt. His face was as round and soft skinned as a baby's, while the fluff of hair on top of his head was as white as an old man's.

"Certainly, Missus." Kolliwobbles beamed at Zara, and then went scampering after Rex and George.

Beatrice's knowledge of magical beings was limited, but she thought Kolliwobbles might be an elf. She had met a few elves and brownies, and she was pretty sure he wasn't a brownie. For one thing, he wasn't wearing brown.

Beatrice glanced at Quincy. "An elf?" she asked.

Quincy grinned and shook his head. "We'd be better off with an elf—they can actually be helpful. But Kolliwobbles is a pixie. He's the nanny," Quincy added, his eyes twinkling.

Kolliwobbles was herding the little boys up the stairs when the youngest—George, Beatrice remembered—turned around and muttered something under his breath. All at once, the doors of the birdcages swung open and flying birds suddenly filled the hall. The sound of so many beating wings was deafening. *And scary*, Beatrice thought, as a huge yellow bird swooped down and barely missed her head.

"*George!*" Zara shouted. "Haven't I told you not to do that? Kolliwobbles, make him reverse the spell. *Kolliwobbles!*"

But Kolliwobbles was nowhere to be seen. Then Beatrice caught sight of a streak of blue in one of the rooms off the hall. Giggling like a small child, the pixie was opening all the cages in there, as well. Soon every bird in the house was free, and everyone was ducking and screaming and bumping into one another. Cayenne was leaping into the air, an expression of ecstasy on her face, as she nearly caught a red-and-green bird that was larger than she was. And Rex, George, and Kolliwobbles were rolling around on the floor laughing themselves silly.

It was only when Xenos went to stand on the stairs and shouted for silence that everyone stopped leaping, ducking, and screaming. They all stood perfectly still—except for Rex, George, and Kolliwobbles, who were still lying on the floor overcome with mirth—while Xenos murmured something that Beatrice couldn't hear. The next instant, all the birds were back in their cages and the doors were firmly closed.

Xenos sighed. Then he looked down at Kolliwobbles, his expression quite stern.

"Kolliwobbles," Xenos said firmly, "this will not do."

Kolliwobbles had stopped giggling. He stood up slowly and hung his head.

"You were hired to keep my grandsons out of trouble," Xenos went on, "not to join them in their escapades. After our last talk, I thought you understood."

"This happens all the time?" Teddy whispered to Quincy.

"Or worse," Quincy replied.

"So why doesn't your grandfather fire him?"

Quincy grinned and said softly, "Because Kolliwobbles has already been fired from every job he's ever had—about fifty of them—and Grandfather doesn't have the heart to let him go."

A subdued and apparently remorseful Kolliwobbles started upstairs with Rex and George. Watching them, Zara ran her hands through her hair, making it look even wilder. She turned to her guests with a wan smile and said, "I'll take you to your rooms."

"Before we go," Beatrice said quickly, "I have a question."

Everyone turned to stare at her, including Miranda, who was looking especially smug.

Beatrice said to Quincy, "Earlier, you seemed to recognize Miranda."

Quincy raised his eyebrows and nodded. "Of course, I recognized her. We grew up in this house together."

Beatrice blinked. "You grew up together?"

"Miranda is my cousin," Quincy said, looking puzzled now. "And yours, too. Didn't you know that?"

Beatrice was too astonished to speak.

"Miranda is my daughter Willow's child," Xenos said as he started down the stairs.

Beatrice couldn't believe this. She looked at Miranda, whose face showed clearly that this was the moment she had been waiting for.

"*Gotcha*," Miranda said softly.

"So what's the big deal?" Ulysses said impatiently. "Miranda is my sister's daughter. I don't know why that should be so shocking."

Because, Beatrice wanted to say, *this girl is awful. Maybe even evil. And she's my cousin.* But she couldn't be Dally Rumpe. Beatrice thought about that for a moment. *Could* she?

"So why did you leave here and go to live in the mortal world?" Teddy demanded.

Miranda's face turned sullen. "Because my parents made me. I sure wouldn't have gone on my own."

"Willow and Ephraim had a very nice gift shop here in town," Xenos said. "But business dropped off—"

"Because of you," Miranda said coldly to Beatrice.

"Miranda," Xenos admonished her. "Anyway, they decided to try opening a shop in the mortal world and, of course, they wanted their daughter with them."

"So now *I* have a question for you," Quincy said to Miranda. "What are you doing back here?"

From the way he spoke, Beatrice had a strong feeling that Quincy was no more fond of Miranda than she was.

Miranda's eyes narrowed. "I'm back to take my rightful place as a Bailiwick witch," she informed him.

Now Zara was looking upset. "Miranda—sweetheart—we've been over this before. You aren't a Bailiwick—well, of course, you *are* a Bailiwick, but your name is Pengilly. So you can't—" She glanced apologetically at Beatrice. "You aren't *allowed* to break Dally Rumpe's spell."

Miranda's eyes were flashing. "That's so *unfair!*" she shouted. "I'm kept from doing what I should be doing—what I'm *entitled* to do—because of a technicality. So my name is Pengilly. *So what?* You said it yourself, Aunt Zara, I'm still a Bailiwick, and I'm four months older than *her*—" Miranda shot Beatrice a furious look, "so that makes *me* the eldest female Bailiwick witch in my generation. *I* should be going after Dally Rumpe."

"Oh, for Pete's sake, Miranda," Ulysses said angrily. "*No one* should be going after Dally Rumpe. If *some* people would just leave well enough alone, we could go back to the way things used to be."

Miranda was standing there with her arms folded across her chest, gritting her teeth. "I'm going to do this," she said savagely.

"What makes you think you can?" Ulysses insisted. "Your mother couldn't!"

Miranda's face turned red and blotchy. She appeared ready to explode. Even Beatrice no longer thought she looked beautiful.

"*Enough!*" Xenos rubbed his face with both hands, as if he were very tired. "I suppose," he said wearily, and turned to look at Beatrice, "you deserve to know this. My sister, Bridget, was the eighth Bailiwick witch to try to break Dally Rumpe's spell. She failed."

"Papa, you don't have to tell her—" Ulysses started.

Xenos waved a hand to silence his son. "My daughter, Willow, was the ninth Bailiwick witch to try. She also failed." Xenos shrugged. "Of course, Willow was more interested in parties and boys than she was in Dally Rumpe's curse, so I don't think she tried very hard."

"Willow didn't care a fig," Ulysses agreed.

"Well, I *do* care," Miranda said stubbornly, scowling at all of them. "And I can't believe my own family doesn't see that I'm the one who should be doing this. *She's* just a Reform witch—and from what I've seen, a total dud in the magic department."

"And you, on the other hand, are a great sorcerer?" Quincy was laughing now. "As I recall, you can only cast one spell, Miranda."

Miranda stood very still, her eyes narrowed and focused on Quincy's face with deadly concentration. "I don't have to listen to this," she said quietly. "And I don't need your permission to do what I want."

With that, Miranda spun around and flounced up the stairs.

No one spoke for a moment, then Quincy looked at Beatrice and said cheerfully, "She never was much fun."

"But—she's my cousin," Beatrice finished lamely.

"You know, Beatrice," Quincy said kindly, "just because she's a Bailiwick—sort of—doesn't mean that she has to be nice."

They were all quiet as they got into the elevator with Zara to go upstairs, an elevator that normally would have elicited comment from Teddy and Cyrus, at least. The brass grillwork on the door formed a design of mermaids and dolphins. But only Sasha seemed to notice, as she scribbled away, muttering, "Life-sized mermaids . . ."

"Beatrice, you'll be with Teddy, and the boys will room together. Peregrine can have his own room," Zara added with a smile for the despondent witch adviser. "And I hope this won't be difficult for you," she said to Sasha, "but I thought you could share a room with Miranda."

Sasha shrugged. "No problem," she said. "Once, on assignment, I had to bunk with trolls."

Zara stopped the elevator on the third floor. Cyrus, who was standing in front, stepped out first. And dropped out of sight!

Beatrice gasped. She stuck her head into the hall and realized that the elevator had stopped a good two feet above the floor. Then she saw Cyrus sprawled across the polished stones. He was holding his leg and moaning softly.

"Oh, my gosh!" Zara said in horror. "He's really hurt, isn't he?"

Beatrice, Teddy, and Ollie leaped out of the elevator and ran to their friend's side.

"Cyrus, are you okay?" Beatrice asked anxiously, kneeling down beside him. "Is it your leg?"

Cyrus's face was contorted with pain. "I think it's broken," he said weakly. And then he passed out.

8

Trapped

Beatrice, Teddy, Ollie, and Cayenne were sitting on a bench outside Cyrus's door when Zara and an elderly physician named Dr. Cattermole emerged.

"Thank goodness his leg isn't broken," Zara said.

"But he has a bad sprain," Dr. Cattermole told them. "I've cast a spell to relieve the pain and reduce the swelling, but he still needs to stay off that ankle a few days."

"Can we see him?" Beatrice asked.

"He's asleep now," the doctor said. "Why don't you wait until morning? But don't worry, your friend is going to be fine."

"Thank you, Doctor," Zara said.

But Dr. Cattermole had already vanished.

"I should see about dinner," Zara said to Beatrice and her friends. "You're probably hungry."

"Not very," Beatrice replied, and Teddy and Ollie shook their heads.

It had been a hard day. First, the balloon crashing, then the charges against Peregrine, and now Cyrus getting hurt. Food was the last thing on their minds.

"I think these accidents are more than a coincidence," Beatrice said.

"Me, too," Ollie agreed.

Zara gave them a startled look. "You mean the elevator? I have to admit, I was wondering about that myself." She frowned. "It's always worked perfectly up to now, and we just had the regular maintenance done a few weeks ago."

"Cyrus falling out of the elevator isn't the only accident we've had today," Ollie said, and proceeded to tell Zara about the balloon going down.

Zara's eyes opened wide with horror as she listened. "Oh, you poor dears!" she exclaimed. "Why didn't you tell us right away? We should have Dr. Cattermole look at you. Oh, this is terrible! I'll call the doctor back—"

"There's no need for that," Beatrice cut in hastily. "We're fine. It's just that *two* accidents in one day seems more than a coincidence."

Zara's worried eyes moved across their faces. "Are you certain you aren't hurt? All right . . . if you're sure. But you lost all your clothes and personal items, didn't you?"

Teddy sighed. "I don't even have a hair dryer."

"Well, I can remedy that," Zara declared. "Give me your sizes."

After she was gone, Beatrice said to Teddy and Ollie, "Cornelius Wrenn had just checked the cord on the balloon and it was working perfectly. Now Aunt Zara says the elevator was working perfectly. And Peregrine's trouble . . . Someone is *doing* all this."

While Beatrice and Teddy were putting on their new clothes the next morning, Teddy said, "I was hoping for something a little more witchy than jeans and T-shirts. We can get this stuff at home."

"I guess Aunt Zara looked at what we had on and tried to duplicate it," Beatrice replied. "And that's fine with me. Witches' robes are hot and get in the way."

After collecting Ollie, they went to the sick room down the hall to look in on Cyrus. He was sitting up in bed wolfing down serpents' eggs and toast.

"You look good," Beatrice said. "Does it hurt much?"

"Not really," Cyrus replied, then a shadow crossed his face. "But how much help can I be to you guys laid up like this? Should I just go home?"

"Not on your life!" Beatrice exclaimed.

"No way," Teddy said. "I'd miss you bossing me around."

"You'll be fine in a few days," Ollie assured him.

"I hope so," Cyrus said, and yawned. "That was a pretty strong spell the doc cast. Think I'll take a nap."

"Good idea," Beatrice said. "We'll come back later."

When they went down to the dining room, Beatrice and her friends found Zara serving breakfast to Quincy and Peregrine.

"Aunt Zara," Beatrice said, "thanks for the clothes."

"You're welcome, darling," Zara replied. "I'm just sorry that you had to begin your stay here with such a terrible experience."

A stack of plates on the server began to arrange themselves around the table.

"Okay, everybody sit down," Zara said. "Have you seen Cyrus? He looks better already, doesn't he? Pour

89

yourselves some dragon's milk and I'll bring in the rest of the food. We're having potato-bug pancakes—have you ever tried them?—scrambled serpents' eggs, and mosquito muffins with wild onion jelly."

"Sounds delicious," Beatrice said, and slid into the chair next to Peregrine. Cayenne took the chair on the other side of the witch adviser.

Looking tired and dejected, Peregrine was pushing food around on his plate but not eating much.

Wanting to comfort him, Beatrice said, "Dr. Featherstone will get to the bottom of this."

"I'm sure she'll try," Peregrine answered forlornly.

Teddy had made a point of sitting next to Quincy. "So where's Miranda?" Teddy asked.

Quincy shrugged and grinned. "Probably upstairs plotting her revenge against me."

"Does she do that?" Beatrice asked.

"Oh, yeah!" Quincy laughed. "Once, when we were little, I snitched a cookie from her—and a week later, she retaliated by pushing me down the stairs. *Thirty-seven* steps. Miranda holds a grudge for a *long* time."

"So her mother was the last Bailiwick witch who tried to break Dally Rumpe's spell?" Beatrice asked as Zara came in carrying a tray heaped with food.

"That's right," Quincy said. "But you heard Grandfather. I don't think Aunt Willow tried very hard. From what I've been told, she went to the first place, saw an enchanted hedge of thorns that seemed impossible to get around, and came home."

"That was in Winter Wood," Teddy said. "It *was* pretty intimidating."

About that time, Miranda appeared in the doorway.

"Well, look at her," Teddy said under her breath. "*She* didn't get jeans."

Miranda was wearing a long black dress cinched in at the waist with a silver belt. On her arm was a wide silver cuff bracelet set with black stones.

"You look very pretty, Miranda," Zara said.

Miranda plucked at her skirt and frowned. "This old thing? But thank goodness I left a few clothes here."

Miranda sat down directly across from Beatrice and fastened her eyes on Beatrice's face. Beatrice wasn't surprised. She had expected the games to continue.

Zara was moving around the table placing small glasses of red liquid in front of each of them.

"Oh, no," Quincy said, "not this stuff again."

Teddy picked up her glass and sniffed. "What is it?"

"Fever Reliever," Zara replied. "One glassful a year protects you from witch fever."

"It tastes terrible," Miranda protested.

"We have an outbreak every spring," Zara said, "so drink up—You, *too*, Quincy."

Beatrice raised her glass and took a big gulp. *That isn't so bad*, she was thinking, and then an awful taste began to spread through her mouth.

Teddy's face screwed up and she made a gagging sound. "It tastes like bitter weeds—only *lots* worse."

Everyone at the table was making a face and reaching for something else to drink.

"Dragon's milk helps," Quincy said, and swallowed a mouthful.

A few minutes later, Sasha came in rubbing her eyes. "Sorry I'm late," she said through a yawn. "I'm not a morning person."

Xenos and Ulysses showed up right behind her.

"You know, Beatrice," Quincy said suddenly, "Grandfather might have something that would help you break the spell on Sea-Dragon Bay. He has a lot of old manuscripts dealing with sea monsters."

Ulysses shot his son an irritated look and proceeded to attack his serpent's eggs as if they could fight back. Xenos just nodded, and said, "I'd be happy for you to see the manuscripts, Beatrice. Angel Crump, my librarian, can help you find anything you need."

"And you might want to talk to Great-aunt Bridget," Quincy went on. "She doesn't see anyone except Grandfather, but she might make an exception with you."

Xenos sat back abruptly in his chair. "That won't be possible," he said tersely. "Bridget hasn't had visitors in forty years."

"That's just the point," Quincy responded. "She's been locked up in that tower feeling guilty and ashamed way too long. Talking to Beatrice might help her."

Xenos's eyes locked with Quincy's. "I said *no*." He spoke quietly, but his tone left no room for discussion.

Just then, Rex and George came racing into the room, still in their nightclothes. Kolliwobbles was right behind them, wearing red pajamas with feet in them. Kolliwobbles was giggling, and Rex and George were screaming, "Help, help! The monsters are after us!"

Xenos and Ulysses looked up and frowned at the same moment.

"*Kolliwobbles!*" Xenos bellowed over the noise his grandsons were making.

The nanny stopped in his tracks and his blue eyes darted to Xenos.

"Did you create monsters to chase them again?" Xenos demanded.

Kolliwobbles dropped his head. "Only *little* monsters," he mumbled.

"I told you not to do that, didn't I?"

Kolliwobbles nodded, looking pathetic.

"Then do away with them right now," Xenos said sternly, "before they're in here having breakfast with us. I'm about to lose my patience, Kolliwobbles. I'll give you one more chance to prove that you can be a positive role model for the boys. Do you understand?"

Kolliwobbles nodded again. Rex and George dashed past him and into the hall, still screaming. Staring down at his skinny feet, the pixie shuffled slowly out of the room.

"I was against hiring him," Ulysses declared.

"Kolliwobbles does keep the boys entertained," Zara said in the nanny's defense. "And he's very creative. He just has a lot of—pent-up energy. Maybe if he got out more . . ." Then an idea seemed to come to her. "Quincy, why don't you give Beatrice and her friends a tour of the town this morning? And you can take your brothers and Kolliwobbles with you."

Quincy frowned. "That sounds good—except for the part about Kolliwobbles and the boys. I refuse to be seen in public with them."

"Peregrine, come with us," Beatrice said as they prepared to leave.

"I don't think so," Peregrine replied listlessly.

"Then I'll show you my library, Peregrine," Xenos said, and his face lit up with pleasure. "I have more than twenty thousand manuscripts, and Angel is in the process of cataloging them all by subject, title, and author. I think you'll find it very interesting."

"Oh, I'm sure," Peregrine said with a noticeable lack of enthusiasm.

"All right then," Beatrice said doubtfully. "We won't be gone long."

"I'm ready," Sasha said brightly, reaching for her pen and notebook.

Miranda scowled. "How long are you going to be tagging around after us, anyway?"

Sasha looked surprised but not particularly offended. "Why, until I've finished my story."

Teddy moved next to Quincy as they started down the street. Beatrice lagged behind, staring beyond the castle at the black tower. It was round and at least a hundred feet tall, reminding Beatrice of a grim sort of lighthouse. Sitting as it was on a narrow strip of sand that jutted out into the bay, the tower was surrounded on three sides by water. Beatrice got a lonely feeling just looking at it.

Then her gaze shifted to the bonfires that stretched out from the tower into the waters of the bay. Their scarlet and yellow flames blazed as high as a two-story house, leaving a smoky haze across the water.

Quincy had come to stand with Beatrice, and the others joined them.

"The shallow water along the beach has always been the safe area," Quincy said. "We grew up knowing that we could swim there without worrying about riptides and sea monsters. But see how the water becomes darker about thirty feet out? That means it's deeper, and we weren't allowed to swim there because the rip currents can be deadly. The sea monsters used to stay in the waters beyond the firedrake islands. But now some of them are slipping past the fires and coming closer to shore."

"Since you came along," Miranda cut in, giving Beatrice a hard look.

Quincy frowned at Miranda. "Will you stop haranguing her?" he demanded. "I mean, if you'd had your way, it would have been *you* going after Dally Rumpe and stirring things up."

"*I* would have done it better and faster," Miranda said crisply, "and it would all be over by now."

"Oh, brother," Teddy muttered.

"Ignore her," Quincy advised Beatrice. "Anyway, do you see that island on the horizon?"

Far out across the bay, Beatrice could just make out what appeared to be rugged peaks rising out of the water. "I see it."

"That's where Ailsa is imprisoned," Quincy said quietly. "It's called Island on the Edge. Because we can't see beyond that point—and no one can sail out there—so Ailsa's island is like the edge of the Earth to us."

"But now Beatrice and her trusty sidekicks are going to fix that," Miranda said sourly.

Teddy shot Miranda an angry look, but Beatrice ignored her and looked again at the tower. There was a door at its base and one small window near the top. Beatrice couldn't be certain at this distance, but she thought she saw movement in the window.

"Why does Bridget live there?" Beatrice asked, staring hard at that window, hoping to see a face.

"Because she failed," Quincy said simply. "I can't begin to understand it myself, but Mother told me that Bridget felt so ashamed when she returned to Sea-Dragon Bay, she couldn't bear to face anyone. So she had that tower built, and took it upon herself to guard the bay and keep the firedrakes burning to scare off the sea monsters. I guess she thought it was the least she could do, since she hadn't been able to reverse Dally Rumpe's spell."

"And she hasn't left the tower in forty years?" Teddy asked. "I can see why she felt bad, but *forty years?*"

"It's incredible, I know," Quincy said. "And she won't see anyone except Grandfather. Once a week, he takes her food and books and anything else she needs. Then he leaves and she's alone again."

"So you've never met her," Beatrice said, feeling an overwhelming sadness for this poor woman.

"No," Quincy said. He paused before adding, "But when I was little, I used to sneak out to the tower at night and look up at the window. Sometimes I'd see her—this small dark figure in the dim candlelight. And once, she waved at me."

Miranda jerked her head around to look at him. "You never told me that," she said, her voice accusing.

Quincy scowled at her. "Why should I have? You considered her a failure, like most of the other witches in this town."

Miranda shrugged. "Well, isn't she?"

"*No*," Quincy said emphatically. "Boy—I don't *blame* Aunt Bridget for staying away from people like you. Come on," he added briskly, "I'll show you guys The Firedrake Inn. It's very nice."

On their way down the street, Ollie pointed out a small sand-colored building with a sign that read: *Sea-Dragon Bay Museum.*

"I'd like to go in there," Ollie said.

"Sure," Quincy said.

"There's nothing worth seeing," Miranda grumbled. "Just a lot of old junk."

Wadsworth Fretwell was squatting in front of the museum sticking plastic flowers into a patch of sand beside the door.

"Hello there, Wadsworth," Quincy said.

Wadsworth scrambled awkwardly to his feet, dropping his trowel and some garish purple flowers in the process. "Oh—Hello, Quincy. What a pleasant surprise. Always nice to see one of the Bailiwicks."

"Doing more good deeds, I see," Quincy said.

Wadsworth glanced at the flowers he had dropped, stooped to retrieve them, and stumbled to his knees. "Well, yes," he said, staggering back up and dusting off his robes, spraying them all with sand. "I try to be helpful."

Quincy said good-bye to the witch and opened the door to the museum. Following him inside, Beatrice saw that they were in a small room lined with glass cases. The museum was deserted except for an old witch asleep at a desk in the corner.

Beatrice blew her bangs aside and leaned down to study a drawing of a giant sea serpent swallowing a ship. *Is this like the serpent that guards Ailsa?* Beatrice wondered, and feeling a creeping uneasiness, quickly moved away.

The others were filing past a wall of drawings and photographs with a banner overhead that read: *Famous Local Witches*. Beatrice joined them. She was reading about Valeska Yule, who turned back the hurricane of 1587 and saved the town, when she heard Ollie ask, "What's downstairs?"

"I've never been down there," Miranda answered, sounding bored. "I suppose we could check it out. It couldn't be any worse than this."

Beatrice noticed Ollie and Miranda descending a narrow staircase, and thought about joining them. But the display of local witches was interesting, and she moved on to the next one: a sad-looking witch named Granville Oxblood, who started the first mail delivery service in the Witches' Sphere in 1402, using vampire bats as carriers. Beatrice read that the service wasn't very popular because the bats kept biting everyone and witches got sick of being turned into vampires.

"Beatrice, have you seen this?" Sasha said at her elbow.

Beatrice looked at the photograph in front of Sasha. It was a picture of an attractive young girl who seemed vaguely familiar. Then Beatrice saw the name beneath the photo and realized why. It was Bridget Bailiwick.

"The eighth Bailiwick witch to fail . . ." Sasha read quickly, her eyes darting ahead. "After losing her nerve,

Bridget returned to Sea-Dragon Bay and no one in town has seen her since . . . the self-designated keeper of the fires . . . continuing her solitary vigil year after year . . ."

Beatrice turned away. The more she heard about Bridget, the sadder she felt. Beatrice wondered if Bridget knew that Beatrice and her friends were here. And if she did, how must she feel about a young witch coming in to do what she, Bridget, had not been able to do?

When they left the museum, Quincy said, "Come on, I'll take you to The Firedrake Inn for a scrumptious lunch."

"That sounds great," Beatrice said, and looked around to see if her friends agreed. That's when she realized that Ollie wasn't with them.

"Miranda, where's Ollie?" Beatrice asked.

"How should I know?"

"You went downstairs with him."

"And left immediately," Miranda said. "Nothing down there but a bunch of old crates. And it was filthy!"

"I'm going to look for him," Beatrice said.

"We'll all go," Quincy said.

As they walked back to the museum, Beatrice heard Miranda muttering, "He's a big boy. I'm sure he can find his way home."

Beatrice felt like turning around and telling Miranda off, once and for all. But she fought the desire to have it out with her cousin because she was beginning to worry about Ollie. Finding him was her only priority at the moment.

Beatrice started walking faster. *He's fine*, she told herself, but her feeling that Ollie was in trouble only seemed to grow.

Beatrice was running when she reached the museum. As Wadsworth Fretwell stared at her, Beatrice jerked the door open and headed for the stairs.

"Beatrice, wait up!"

Beatrice heard Teddy's voice, but she was already clattering down the narrow staircase to the cellar and didn't respond.

At the bottom of the steps was a heavy wooden door. Beatrice yanked on the old-fashioned iron handle, but the door wouldn't budge.

"Here, let me," Quincy said. He pulled hard, but it didn't move.

Beatrice looked at Miranda, who was standing halfway up the stairs. "Did this door open before?" she asked.

"How do you think we got in?"

"Well, it won't open now," Quincy said.

Beatrice held up a hand. "Listen," she said abruptly.

In the silence that followed, they could hear faint knocking on the other side of the door.

"Ollie!" Beatrice called. "Ollie, are you in there?"

They heard a voice in response, but it was too muffled to make out the words.

Beatrice glanced at Quincy. "He's in there, and he can't get out." Then she glanced down and saw water seeping out from under the door. "Look!" she shouted.

When Quincy saw the water, the muscles in his face tightened. "Some of these cellars flood during high tide."

"When is high tide?" Teddy asked sharply.

Quincy glanced at his watch. "Right about now," he said.

"Oh, no," Beatrice said softly. She looked around frantically. "We have to find a way to break through the door."

"I'll go get the museum guy," Sasha said, and took off up the stairs, nearly knocking Miranda down in her haste.

Beatrice found a pile of discarded table legs in the corner. She picked up one of the heavy legs and started bashing the door with it, but the door didn't give an inch. And the floor was now covered with water.

Teddy and Quincy had both grabbed the door handle and were pulling as hard as they could.

"There's no lock," Quincy grunted, still pulling, "unless it's inside."

"But Ollie wouldn't have locked himself in!" Beatrice protested. She heard the panic in her voice and took a deep breath. She had to stay calm and keep a clear head. She had to *think!*

"What's all the banging and yelling?" came a querulous voice from overhead.

The old witch, who had been asleep, came stomping down the stairs toward them. He didn't look happy.

"Our friend is locked in here!" Beatrice shouted, forgetting that she was supposed to stay calm.

"Impossible," the old witch responded. "There's no lock on the door."

"Then the door's *stuck*," Beatrice said. "And water's coming in."

"Yep," the old witch agreed. "Always does at high tide."

Beatrice's heart was pounding. "How high does the water get inside that room?" she demanded.

"To the ceiling."

Beatrice's desperate eyes met Teddy's. "Then he'll *drown!*"

"Listen to me," Sasha said fiercely to the old witch. "You have to get our friend *out of there!*"

He yanked on the handle and then shrugged. "Well, I don't know how. It's not locked, but it won't open."

Beatrice made a sound of denial in her throat. She lunged against the door, hitting it hard with her shoulder. But the solid old door held fast.

"Wait," Quincy said, and grabbed Beatrice before she could throw herself at the door again. "I can get him out."

Beatrice looked at Quincy, her expression at once incredulous and hopeful. "You can?"

Quincy nodded. "Yeah. Just stand back."

And then Quincy began to chant:

> *Spirits of the sky and sea,*
> *Grant my wish—so mote it be!*
> *By sunlight's glow or moonlight's beam,*
> *Turn this door to pastry cream.*

Suddenly the door was transformed from thick wood to whipped cream. Then a gush of water broke through the frothy confection, melting it and soaking Beatrice and the others. Just as Miranda screamed in fury, Beatrice caught sight of a drenched Ollie standing in the doorway.

Beatrice stepped toward him, smiling. Then, without realizing it was going to happen, she started to cry.

"It's okay," Ollie said. He tried to grin at her, but it came out a little lopsided. "I thought I was a goner there for a while—the water just kept climbing higher and higher!—but I'm fine now."

"What happened?" Teddy demanded. "Did you lock the door?"

"No," Ollie said, appearing puzzled. "Miranda left and I snooped around a little, didn't find anything, and started to leave. But the door wouldn't open."

"I told you," the old witch said gruffly, "that door doesn't lock!"

"Then it was magic," Beatrice said softly. Her eyes met Ollie's. "Or another coincidence?"

Ollie shook his head. He looked angry. "It was no coincidence," he said.

Now that she was certain that Ollie was all right, Teddy turned admiring eyes to Quincy. "You're a hero," she said. "And what a cool spell."

Quincy grinned, but he looked a little embarrassed. "I can only cast one kind of spell," he admitted. "It was tough growing up. I never wanted the other kids at the witch academy to know that I could do it."

"Do *what*?" Teddy asked.

Quincy's face turned pink. "What I just did. Turn an inanimate object into a dessert."

Miranda was sniggering, and Beatrice made a point of ignoring her.

"Ollie would have drowned without your spell," Beatrice said to Quincy. "I think it's the best spell I've ever heard."

Teddy, however, was glaring at Miranda. "You left right before the door stuck," Teddy said. "A little odd, don't you think?"

Miranda's lips curved into her trademark half smile. "I didn't do it," she answered smugly. "So there must be someone else who wants you all to leave."

Just then, Wadsworth Fretwell's face appeared over the stair railing. "I heard yelling. Is something wrong?"

"You're a little late, Fretwell," the old museum witch said gruffly. "Nobody here needs one of your good deeds. At least, not anymore."

Wadsworth Fretwell looked hurt. "I just try to be helpful," he said.

9

The Witch
Who Failed

No one wanted to go to The Firedrake Inn for lunch. They were all soaking wet and not feeling very festive.

"Let's go home and Mother will fix us something," Quincy said.

"And we can check on Cyrus and Peregrine," Beatrice added.

"Peregrine's probably still in the library," Quincy said, grinning, as they entered the castle. "When Grandfather starts showing off his beloved manuscripts, he can go on and on."

"Well, I for one have had my fill of dusty old rooms," Miranda said. "I'm going to take a long bath."

"Sounds like a good idea," Sasha responded. Then she looked quickly at Beatrice. "But if anything exciting happens, come get me, okay?"

"All we need is more excitement," Ollie said grimly.

Quincy started for the elevator, but Beatrice said, "Can't we take the stairs? It might be—safer."

Quincy smiled. "Yeah, I see your point. All right, follow me."

A narrow stone staircase led down, down, down, and never seemed to end.

"Where is the library, anyway?" Teddy asked him. "At the bottom of the ocean?"

"In the dungeon," Quincy said. "When The Sandcastle was first built—oh, six or seven hundred years ago—the first Bailiwicks kept their enemies in chains down here."

"How quaint," Beatrice murmured.

They had finally come to the bottom of the stairs and were standing in a long hallway lit by torches. The flames cast fitful shadows across the stone walls, and the air smelled damp and moldy.

"It's kind of creepy down here," Teddy said, her voice hushed.

"Don't let Grandfather hear you say that," Quincy said cheerfully.

He pulled open a heavy door, and light poured out into the dimly-lit hall, its unexpected warmth drawing them into Xenos Bailiwick's library.

"This is much better," Beatrice said, looking around the vast room.

Shelves lined every wall from the stone floor to the high vaulted ceiling, and most of the shelves were crammed with leather-bound books and manuscripts. Down the center of the room were a half-dozen library tables, all covered with stacks of books and papers.

At the far end of the room, Beatrice saw Uncle Xenos and Peregrine, their heads together as they studied a scroll spread out across one of the tables. Angel Crump sat at a nearby desk writing in a large book.

At their approach, Angel looked up, quilled pen poised, and glared at them. Cayenne's attention was caught by the long black feather in the librarian's hand, and she pounced. Inkwell, pen, and book went flying.

Xenos's head jerked up when Angel cried out, his eyes quickly taking in the librarian's furious face and Beatrice's horrified one, the ink-splattered papers, and the trail of black paw prints that led under the desk.

"It's no disaster, Angel," Xenos said mildly, and gave Beatrice a reassuring smile.

"But that—that—*cat* spilled ink all over everything," the librarian sputtered. "I nearly had this translation complete, and now you can't even read it! I'll have to start all over."

Beatrice had dropped to her knees and was hauling an unwilling Cayenne out from under the desk while she repeated several times how sorry she was.

"Accidents happen," Xenos replied gently. "Don't worry about it."

As Beatrice scrambled to her feet, holding her disgruntled cat, she saw that Peregrine was watching it all—and he was actually *smiling*. Beatrice blew her bangs out of her eyes and smiled back.

"I want you to meet the most dedicated librarian in the Sphere," Xenos was saying, while Angel mopped up ink and glowered. "This is—"

But before he could finish, the library door swung open and banged against the wall. Everyone jumped. A tall, barrel-chested witch in black robes stood in the doorway for an instant, then took long, unhurried strides toward them.

Xenos's eyes were narrowed as they looked the newcomer up and down. It was obvious that he didn't welcome the intrusion.

"May I help you?" Xenos asked, his voice cordial but noticeably cool. "I am Xenos Bailiwick—"

"Right, right," the witch in black said with a dismissive wave of his hand. "I know who you are. I know who all of you are." His hawkish, thin- lipped face seemed incapable of smiling. "I have photographs," he added, his voice heavy with importance, and pointed to the bulging briefcase he carried. "As well as dossiers on each of you."

Xenos was frowning. "Just who are you?" he demanded.

"My name is Junius Sternbuckle," the witch replied. "I've just arrived from the Witches' Institute, and I'm here to conduct an investigation."

Everyone's eyes turned to Peregrine. The witch adviser seemed to shrink down into his robes, and Beatrice could see his legs start to tremble beneath the brown fabric. But Peregrine still managed to take a wobbly step forward and say in a weak voice, "Then you'll be wanting to talk to me."

"Eventually," Junius Sternbuckle replied, his tone living up to his name. "When *I* decide to," he added, as if to let them know right away who was in charge around here. "I'll be talking to all of you. But first, I want to get settled in."

Xenos appeared uncertain. "You plan to stay *here?*"

"Correct." The investigator looked around, and added, "This room will suit me just fine. And while I'm here, it will be strictly off limits to everyone else. Privacy is crucial in my business."

Xenos blanched. "But this is my library," he protested feebly. "There's important work going on—"

"Nothing more important than an investigation, surely," Junius Sternbuckle said, his expression more severe than ever. "Is there a room nearby with a bed?"

Xenos sighed and his shoulders slumped. "There's a storeroom in the back. I'll have it cleaned up and a bed moved in."

"And about my meals," the investigator went on. "I'll want them served promptly at seven, one, and seven. Hot meals, no sandwiches. I'll want a snack at eleven. And, oh, yes—inform the cook that I can't abide chives."

After looking in on Cyrus, and seeing that he was asleep, Beatrice, Teddy, and Ollie went to Beatrice and Teddy's room to talk. They sat on the floor and leaned against the beds. Cayenne stretched out for a much-needed nap on Beatrice's pillow.

"You know," Beatrice said, "so much has been happening, we haven't had time to even think about Dally Rumpe's spell. We need to come up with a plan."

Ollie nodded. "It's been one terrible thing after another, all right. And now this Sternbuckle guy acts like we're at his beck and call. He told me to come to the dungeon—I mean, library—at two o'clock."

"He has me down for three," Teddy said. She grimaced. "I'm not looking forward to being grilled."

"Well, I'm supposed to see him in—" Beatrice glanced at her watch, "twenty minutes. And I'm going to tell him that Peregrine is above suspicion, that I'd trust him with my life. And *have*."

Ollie looked troubled. "I don't think Sternbuckle cares about our opinions. He's looking for facts."

"And the fact *is*," Beatrice said hotly, "that Peregrine's innocent. I wonder if Dr. Featherstone has learned who made the accusations."

"I'd be willing to bet it's the same person who locked me in that cellar," Ollie said darkly, "and caused Cyrus's accident."

"And made the balloon go down," Teddy added. "And you know who I'd put my money on? Miranda!"

Beatrice frowned. "She's not very nice," Beatrice admitted, "but—"

"I know, she's family," Teddy interrupted. "But you can't let that cloud your judgment, Beatrice. Dally Rumpe can take on any form he chooses. And Miranda is ambitious. She wants fame and power."

Ollie raised his eyebrows. "You mean, like you."

Teddy shot him an irritated look. "But I'm not ruthless! And I think Miranda Pengilly would do just about anything to get what she wants."

"What about Sasha?" Ollie said suddenly. "Maybe she isn't a reporter at all. She could be using that as a cover, just to get close to us."

"True," Beatrice said. "But she wasn't anywhere near the cellar when you got locked in. She was with me the whole time."

"Okay, then," Teddy said briskly. "What about Wadsworth Fretwell? He's strange, to say the least, and we don't know anything about him."

"Except that he's the clumsiest witch I've ever seen," Ollie said.

"And he's positively obsessed with doing good deeds," Teddy added.

Just then, there was a knock on the door.

"Come in," Beatrice called out.

It was Quincy. "Okay if I join you?" he asked.

"Sure," Beatrice said. "We were just trying to figure out who wants to do us in."

Quincy sank to the floor—next to Teddy, Beatrice noticed.

"So who have you thought of so far?" Quincy asked.

"Miranda, Sasha, and Wadsworth Fretwell." Teddy ticked off the names on her fingers.

"I can see why you'd think of Miranda," Quincy said. "She's pretty heartless. But I can't be objective about her. She's almost like a sister."

"The old Bailiwick loyalty again," Teddy muttered.

Quincy smiled. "I guess so. Anyway, back to your list. I wouldn't have thought of Sasha. She actually seems pretty nice, but not *too* nice. Now Wadsworth Fretwell could be capable of anything. Or maybe not. He's such a doofus."

Beatrice laughed. "Well, the next name on the list should be Angel Crump. He has a thoroughly nasty disposition."

"Especially after Cayenne dumped ink on his manuscript." Teddy's eyes twinkled as she reached out to rub the cat's belly.

Cayenne opened one eye and gave Teddy a reproachful look.

"Sorry," Teddy muttered to the cat. "Let's definitely add Angel to the list. He was a *monster* for getting so upset over one little accident."

"What do you know about Angel?" Ollie asked Quincy.

"Well, he's loyal to my grandfather," Quincy said, "probably because Grandfather gave him a job and treats him with respect. No one else in town has much to do with him. See, Angel's past is kind of murky."

Beatrice looked at him with interest. "Tell us."

"He was adopted by this local couple," Quincy said. "Kemp and Yedda Crump. They were just ordinary witches, and everybody was happy for them when they adopted the baby. They called him their little angel—that's how he got his name—but right away, everybody realized that this baby was anything but an angel. He bit people and screamed his head off when he didn't get his way. And as he got older, he turned really mean. Parents wouldn't let their kids play with him, and he was kicked out of the witch academy for turning the headmaster into a goat. Finally, when Angel was thirteen, his parents moved away."

Beatrice blinked. "And left him here?"

"Yep," Quincy said. "They just moved out in the middle of the night without telling anyone where they were going. People said they left to get away from Angel. That's when Grandfather started looking out for him, and eventually put him in charge of his library. Angel *is* very smart," Quincy admitted. "But no one in the family except Grandfather can stand him."

"So we don't have a clue who Angel really is," Ollie said. "He may just be a librarian with a lousy personality, or he could be—"

"Dally Rumpe," Teddy finished softly.

Beatrice opened the door to the library and stuck her head in cautiously. Junius Sternbuckle had set up his interview area at a table just inside the door.

"Come in, Ms. Bailiwick," the investigator said impatiently. "We mustn't waste time. I have a lot of people to talk to."

Beatrice walked over to the table and sat down across from him. Her heart was skipping around a little and she took a deep breath to calm herself.

Junius Sternbuckle's sharp eyes scanned a sheet of paper in his hand. Beatrice tried to see what was on the paper, but he seemed to be deliberately concealing it. Finally, he looked up, his lips pressed together in a hard line.

"Let me begin by saying that all I want from you are answers to my questions," the investigator said curtly. "I already know that you like your witch adviser and want to defend him. *Don't!*"

Beatrice felt her temper beginning to flare, but she was determined to control it. Getting angry wouldn't help Peregrine, so she took another breath and said quickly, "I understand."

"This is your third trip to the Witches' Sphere," he said. It wasn't a question, but Beatrice nodded and said, "Yes."

"And Peregrine accompanied you each time."

"Yes."

"Did you notice anything different about him on this trip?"

Beatrice thought for a moment before answering, "No, Peregrine is always pretty much the same."

Junius Sternbuckle gave her a shrewd look. "How about what he was wearing?"

"He always wears the same brown robes," Beatrice said, and then stopped. She remembered the new hat. And the watch and shoes.

The investigator's eyes bore into her face. "Well, Ms. Bailiwick, was there something different about his apparel?"

Someone has already told him, Beatrice thought. She could see how this would look to old Sternbuckle—a gold watch, expensive shoes and hat—the kinds of things Peregrine might buy with money from Dally Rumpe.

"Ms. Bailiwick," Junius Sternbuckle said sharply, "please answer my question."

"Peregrine had a few new things," Beatrice said, and added quickly, "but they were gifts."

"What were these items?"

"A hat, a watch, and shoes," Beatrice replied miserably.

"Were these items expensive, Ms. Bailiwick?"

"I don't know how much they cost," Beatrice replied. That much, at least, was true.

"Let me rephrase the question," the investigator said with a touch of impatience in his voice. "Did the gifts *appear* to be of good quality? For example, was the watch made of gold?"

Beatrice sighed. "I guess so."

"And did Peregrine tell you who sent him the gifts?"

This was going to sound *very* bad. "He didn't know," Beatrice mumbled.

"You mean the gifts came from an anonymous source?" Junius Sternbuckle said, pretending to be surprised and puzzled. "Was there no card?"

Beatrice was liking this witch less by the moment. "The card was signed 'From your secret admirer.'"

"My, my," Junius Sternbuckle said. "Someone must admire Peregrine very much indeed to give him a gold watch!"

Beatrice was counting slowly to ten when the investigator asked his next question.

"And where are these items now?"

"I suppose they're in Peregrine's room," Beatrice said. Then she remembered—the hat and the watch were lost when the balloon went down. "No, that's not true," she corrected herself. "Peregrine lost the hat and the watch when our hot-air balloon made a crash landing in the bay. I'm not sure about the shoes."

"So Peregrine has disposed of the items," Junius Sternbuckle murmured, and scribbled something down.

"*No!*" Beatrice exclaimed. "You make it sound like he was destroying evidence. I just told you—we were in a terrible accident. We all lost clothes and things."

The investigator stood up abruptly. "That's all for now, Ms. Bailiwick. I may have additional questions later."

Beatrice got slowly to her feet. "But—"

"I *said*, that's all."

Beatrice felt terrible as she made the long climb up to the first floor. Junius Sternbuckle had misinterpreted everything she said. And those gifts really made Peregrine look bad. Beatrice was certain that Sternbuckle had known about the gifts before talking to her. But who could have told him?

She ran into Quincy in the front hall. "Quincy, do you know if Junius Sternbuckle talked to anyone before me?"

"I saw Miranda coming up from the dungeon a couple of minutes before you went down there." Quincy gave her a questioning look. "Is something wrong?"

"No, nothing's wrong," Beatrice replied.

So Miranda told Sternbuckle about Peregrine's new stuff, Beatrice thought. But that still didn't prove she was Dally Rumpe.

Quincy was studying her face. "What's going on?"

Beatrice's reply was interrupted by pounding on the front door.

"What in the world?" Quincy muttered, and started for the door.

Xenos stuck his head out of his study. "What's all that racket?" he demanded.

Quincy opened the door, and a big red-faced man stood there.

"Oh, Mr. Skeggs," Quincy said. "Won't you come in?"

"That was my intent," the man replied, and stomped into the hall. Beatrice had no idea who he was, but she could tell that he was angry.

"What brings you here, Dashiell?" Xenos asked as he came out to meet the man.

"Trouble," Mr. Skeggs snapped.

Xenos looked surprised. "I thought business was still pretty good at the pet store."

"It was until those grandsons of yours came in today," the man said. "With that pixie."

Xenos frowned, then sighed. "What happened?" he asked.

"One of them—the pixie, I suspect—turned all my hamsters into skunks. *That's* what happened!"

About that time, Xenos began to sniff the air. He caught a whiff of something that made him back off.

"You see?" Dashiell Skeggs said in fury. "Skunks! The whole store and everything in it—including *me*—*smells like skunks!*"

Then the man saw Beatrice and his face turned a deeper shade of red. "And it's all her fault! Our bad luck's multiplying now that *she's* here."

Beatrice was feeling really low. She had almost decided to skip dinner and sulk in her room, but Teddy and Ollie wouldn't allow it.

"They can't blame you for *skunks*," Ollie insisted.

"And you can't hide away," Teddy said. "That's what Miranda wants."

Yes, Beatrice thought, *Miranda would love to see me give up.* With that thought, Beatrice washed her hands and followed Teddy and Ollie downstairs for dinner.

They ran into Zara outside the dining room. "This just came for you, Beatrice," Zara said, and handed Beatrice a cream-colored envelope.

Teddy and Ollie looked on with interest as Beatrice opened the letter.

"Who's it from?" Teddy asked.

Beatrice read the brief note quickly, then raised her eyes. "Listen to this," she said quietly. And then she read the message aloud.

Dear Beatrice,

I would like for you to come visit me. Is eight o'clock tomorrow night convenient for you and your friends? Please ask Quincy to come, as well. I will leave the door unlocked.

With best regards,
Bridget
(the eighth witch to fail)

10

Bridget's Story

eatrice, Ollie, and Teddy pulled Quincy aside
after dinner and showed him the note from
Bridget.

"She wants *me* to come?" Quincy looked surprised.
Then he grinned. "So she *did* see me watching her when I
was a kid. She knew who I was."

"Don't you think your grandfather talks about all of
you when he visits Bridget?" Beatrice asked.

"Probably so," Quincy said thoughtfully. "Since
Grandfather never talks about *her*, it didn't occur to me
that she might know a lot about *me*." Then he frowned.
"Speaking of Grandfather, he's not going to like us going
to see her, even if she *did* invite us. So we can't tell him. If
Aunt Bridget decides to fill him in, that's her business."

"Okay," Beatrice agreed. "And let's not get Sasha
involved in this, either. I don't think she'd write anything
mean, but there's no need to have Bridget's name all over
the newspapers."

Quincy flashed Beatrice a grateful look. "You're right.
Aunt Bridget went through enough forty years ago."

"Do you realize," Teddy said suddenly, "that we've made it through an entire afternoon and evening without anything disastrous happening?"

Ollie grinned. "Yeah, *somebody's* falling down on the job."

"So we finally have time to talk about Dally Rumpe's spell," Beatrice said quietly as they started up the stairs. "Why don't we go to Ollie's room and start brainstorming?" She looked at Quincy. "You know about the tides and the geography of Sea-Dragon Bay, so maybe you can help us."

"Sure," Quincy agreed. "I want to help."

They were halfway up the stairs to the second floor when Beatrice happened to look down and saw Junius Sternbuckle striding toward the front door.

"Look," she whispered. "He's going out."

The others stopped and watched as the investigator closed the door behind him.

Ollie gave Beatrice a quizzical look. "What are you thinking?"

"That Sternbuckle might have information about who filed the charges against Peregrine," Beatrice said. "I wonder if we should . . ."

"Look through his stuff," Ollie finished, and grinned. "Beatrice Bailey, I believe you're developing a criminal mind. Could it be the company you've been keeping?"

Beatrice's face turned pink, but her tone was unyielding when she said, "That investigator hasn't left us a lot of choices. He's already decided that Peregrine's guilty!"

"He has," Teddy agreed.

"But we'd better hurry," Beatrice said. "Sternbuckle may not be gone long."

"Then on to the dungeon," Quincy said with a reckless smile, and started down the stairs.

The hall to the library seemed even creepier at night. Long shadows played against the torchlit walls, suggesting human—and inhuman—forms. Beatrice would catch movement in the corner of her eye and freeze, certain that Junius Sternbuckle was lurking in the shadows waiting to grab them. Even Cayenne appeared subdued and was content to lie quietly in Beatrice's arms. But Quincy, who had roamed these corridors since childhood, moved confidently through the gloom without appearing to give it a thought.

They came to the door of the library and Quincy pulled it open. Beatrice hadn't noticed before the agonized groan the door made as it slid across the stone floor. The sound was so loud, she was certain they must be able to hear it upstairs.

The investigator had left the lights on, but the room seemed to have lost its warmth and no longer welcomed them. Beatrice chided herself for being fanciful. Except for Junius Sternbuckle's briefcase and stacks of his papers, the library looked just the same. But it *felt* different, as if the investigator's stern presence still lingered in the air.

"I'll start with the briefcase," Ollie said. "Teddy, why don't you look through those papers?"

"I can help with that," Quincy said to Teddy.

All that was left to search was the storeroom, where Junius Sternbuckle would be sleeping. "He may keep private papers back there," Beatrice said. "I'll look."

Only one light burned on a small table beside the bed, leaving most of the room in deep shadow. Beatrice felt a shiver dart up her spine, but she shook off her feelings of apprehension and walked in.

There was a small suitcase lying closed on the bed. Cayenne leaped from Beatrice's arms to the bed and stared at the suitcase.

"I should open it, right?" Beatrice asked the cat. "Okay, here goes."

She unzipped the lid and lifted it. A pair of striped pajamas was folded neatly on top and rolled-up socks had been stuffed at one end. All of a sudden, Beatrice felt a strong distaste for what she was doing. She was invading this witch's privacy and that wasn't right. But then she thought of Peregrine—and saw the look of utter disbelief on his face when he first learned he had been suspended—and Beatrice's jaw tightened. She searched the suitcase quickly—finding nothing more interesting than underwear and toothpaste.

Beatrice yanked open the drawer in the bedside table. It was empty. She looked under pillows and even got down on her hands and knees to peer under the bed. Nothing. Feeling disappointed, but also glad to be able to get out of there, Beatrice started for the door.

"Come on, Cay," she said over her shoulder, and then stopped.

That's odd, Beatrice thought. The door was closed, and she distinctly remembered leaving it open.

Beatrice's heart began to beat fast. Her hand felt sweaty as she grabbed the knob. She knew even before she tried, that it wouldn't turn, that the door was stuck fast and wouldn't open. And she was right.

Fear welled up inside her. She resisted the urge to scream, even as she realized that this was just like Ollie being locked in the cellar!

Beatrice looked around anxiously. At least she couldn't see any water coming in. But then she heard movement in the far corner of the room. It was just a soft scratching sound, but loud enough to cause Cayenne to sit at attention and pivot her ears toward it.

Then Beatrice heard a low, drawn-out growl, and realized that it was coming from Cayenne. The cat was standing up on the bed now, her long fur fluffed out until she looked twice her normal size.

The scratching grew louder, clearly audible even over Beatrice's pounding heart. And then she saw them. Dark bodies as large as a cat's. A dozen or more, skittering along the wall. And she could see the skinny, wormlike tails trailing behind them as they ran, their whiskers glistening as the light caught them. Rats! Huge ugly *rats!*

Beatrice stepped back involuntarily, just as she saw Cayenne crouch down, positioning herself to pounce. Beatrice screamed, "*No*, Cayenne! They'll hurt you."

Beatrice grabbed the cat and started backing toward the door, her eyes glued to the creatures along the wall. Except they were moving away from the wall now, out from the deep shadows, and she could see them more clearly— whiskers twitching, beady eyes glinting. And she knew that they could see her, as well. They turned toward her, and in one terrifying instant, seemed to shoot across the floor.

Beatrice didn't have time to work it all out in her mind, but she knew at a basic, instinctual level that these enormous rats meant to attack. This time, Beatrice didn't try to suppress the scream rising in her throat. And when she felt something heavy strike her foot, she lifted her face to the ceiling and howled.

Cayenne was flailing in her arms, determined to be released. Beatrice was just as determined to hold her. They struggled as Beatrice's eyes darted around the room in search of the rats—and Cayenne won. Beatrice felt the cat's silky body slip through her hands, and heard the thump as Cayenne hit the floor.

Beatrice saw in horror that her cat was surrounded by those horrible creatures. They were stalking Cayenne, their nails clicking against the floor, their fierce pointed faces moving closer and closer—

Out of desperation, Beatrice lunged! She fell to the floor, grabbing for Cayenne and imagining all those rats swarming over her body. But despite her size, Cayenne was light on her feet and managed to evade Beatrice's grasp. The cat was going after the rats! Beatrice saw it all in a confusing flash—rats turning, their tails and back feet flying through the air, with Cayenne in close pursuit.

Beatrice scrambled to her feet and moved toward the wall where Cayenne had cornered her prey. Beatrice was astounded. The rats were all clustered together, a dark looming mass so much larger than Beatrice's cat—and Cayenne, the pampered house cat suddenly turned tiger, was managing to hold them at bay with a low-pitched growl.

Then one of the rats rose slowly to its back feet and made an ominous hissing sound in Cayenne's direction. As if on cue, the remaining rats drew themselves up to their full height and hissed in unison. Beatrice felt a moment of panic, realizing that these disgusting creatures meant to come after her cat again. But then she heard a sudden commotion behind her—people were stampeding into the room, shouting out her name—and the startled rats were making a desperate run for an open vent in the wall.

As the last of the rats disappeared, Beatrice seized Cayenne before the cat could follow them into the vent. She turned around, shaking and white-faced, to see Teddy, Ollie, and Quincy standing there. They were quiet now, and looking at her with expressions of alarm and confusion.

"Those things that went into the wall—" Teddy said, her voice laced with dread, "were they *rats?*"

Not trusting herself to speak, Beatrice nodded.

"And it was Cayenne that sent them running?" Ollie asked.

"Yes." Beatrice cleared her throat, then looked down at Cayenne, who was nestled serenely in her arms. "The rats were after *me*, but Cayenne jumped down in the middle of them. She was so fierce!" Beatrice stroked the cat lovingly and Cayenne began to purr. Then Beatrice looked up. "The door wouldn't open—it was the same thing that happened to you, Ollie. I know I didn't close it, but it was stuck, and the rats were coming toward me—"

Teddy reached out and touched Beatrice's arm. "We heard you screaming," she said gently. "And we found the door stuck. So Superwitch here," she added with a grin in Quincy's direction, "worked his magic."

Beatrice looked at the door—or what had once been a door and was now only an empty doorframe. Beatrice peered closer. A doorframe with some yellow goop dripping from it to the floor.

Beatrice frowned. "What's the yellow stuff?"

Quincy looked embarrassed. "Lemon meringue pie," he mumbled, and dropped his eyes.

"If you're okay," Ollie said to Beatrice, "we'd better get out of here."

"Right." What with the rats and the stuck door, Beatrice had momentarily forgotten why they were here. And who might come in and discover them at any moment!

"Did you find anything?" Beatrice asked as they hurried out of the room.

"Nothing," Ollie said. "What about you?"

"Not a thing."

"So *this* was a waste of our time," Teddy said.

Beatrice glanced over her shoulder as they were leaving the library. "How do we explain the door being gone?"

"I'll say my magic got out of hand," Quincy said with a grin. "My folks won't have any trouble believing that."

"But you weren't supposed to be down here," Teddy reminded him.

"I'll say—the door was squeaky—and I came down to oil it."

"With lemon meringue pie," Beatrice muttered.

They made it upstairs and into Ollie's room without anyone seeing them. Beatrice promptly collapsed on Ollie's bed and Cayenne curled up in the crook of her arm. "That's my brave girl," Beatrice crooned.

Teddy, Ollie, and Quincy were all smiling at her.

"Well, this proves it," Beatrice said. "Two stuck doors would be way too much of a coincidence. Someone definitely wants us out of here."

"Let's go over that list of suspects again," Ollie said.

The next morning, Cyrus hobbled down to breakfast.

"Should you be up so soon?" Zara asked with concern.

"Shouldn't you be using crutches?" This was from Beatrice.

"Put your leg up on the chair," Teddy ordered. "Your ankle needs to be elevated."

"All this for a sprained ankle?" Miranda demanded.

"Actually, it doesn't hurt much now," Cyrus said. "And the swelling's gone. I figured I could go out with you guys today."

"Not on your life," Zara responded. "Maybe tomorrow, if you're *much* better. But today, young man, you're going to help me in the kitchen."

Cyrus looked startled. "You mean, *cook?*"

"That's right," Zara said. "I'm planning a special dinner."

Now Cyrus was definitely wary. "What are you cooking?"

"My famous black-widow soup for starters. Then I thought we'd have Three-C salad—that's crickets, cockroaches, and cutworms—and silverfish with noodles." Zara was beaming. "And for dessert, bloodsucker pie! What do you think?"

Cyrus's face was very pale. "I think I'm not quite as well as I thought at first," he mumbled.

"Then you can just sit on a stool and watch *me* cook," Zara said.

Beatrice was trying hard not to laugh, but then she noticed that Cyrus was turning faintly green.

"Aunt Zara, maybe Cyrus should take it easy for one more day," Beatrice said quickly. "But the rest of us can help you. We don't have any plans for the day." *Until we meet Bridget at eight tonight*, she thought.

"I don't cook," Miranda said flatly.

"I think I'll go out and interview some locals," Sasha remarked. And with a disappointed look in Beatrice's direction, she added, "There doesn't seem to be much happening around here."

About that time, Ulysses came into the dining room. He didn't look happy.

"I've just had a complaint from that investigator," he said curtly. "Can anyone explain how his door happened to disappear?"

Quincy started in with a story about the door needing oil, but under his father's frosty gaze, Quincy was doing more stammering than convincing.

Finally, Beatrice said, "Quincy, don't try to defend me. I was down there looking for information that might help clear Peregrine."

The witch adviser's head jerked up and he looked at Beatrice in amazement.

"I know it was wrong," Beatrice went on swiftly, "and I'll apologize to Mr. Sternbuckle. I didn't find anything, anyway," she added with a regretful glance at Peregrine.

"But you tried," Peregrine said, his eyes brimming. "You cared enough to try."

Ulysses was looking at Beatrice with a mixture of disbelief and fury. He appeared ready to explode.

"Wait a minute," Ollie said suddenly. "It wasn't only Beatrice. I was there, too. And I think you should know, Mr. Bailiwick, that we had another strange thing happen last night."

Then Ollie started telling them about the door being stuck, and Beatrice spilled out the story of the rats—and before long, Teddy and Quincy were adding their input and incriminating themselves, as well.

"This is terrible!" Zara exclaimed. "But I don't understand it. You expect to have rats in these old castles, so we had heavy steel vents installed to keep them out."

"The vent was missing," Beatrice informed her.

Ulysses was glowering at Beatrice. "Well, if you hadn't been snooping around down there—"

"Ulysses, for pity's sake," Zara snapped. "This is no time to chastise them. They've had a frightening experience. And in our home!"

Ulysses glared at her, and then at the rest of them, but he didn't say any more.

"That was pretty slick," Quincy murmured to Beatrice as they left the dining room. "Mother isn't even mad. I could take lessons from you."

It was nearly eight o'clock and already dark when Beatrice, Teddy, Ollie, and Quincy arrived at the base of the black tower. Cayenne was perched on Beatrice's shoulder.

They had shown Bridget's note to Cyrus, and he had wanted desperately to come along. But Beatrice had pointed out diplomatically that there would be a lot of steps to climb, and if Cyrus wanted to be well to go with them to Ailsa's island, he shouldn't push it. Cyrus had reluctantly agreed.

Now Beatrice threw back her head and looked up the side of the tower. A soft light glowed in the window at the top.

"Shall we go in?" Beatrice asked, feeling a little weak in the knees. She had been wondering all day how Bridget felt about her being here. This might be an uncomfortable meeting.

"Let's do it," Quincy said briskly, and opened the door.

Lanterns lit the interior, and Beatrice saw immediately that she had been right. There *were* a lot of steps. A spiral staircase filled the center of the tower, gradually disappearing into darkness overhead.

The stone steps were narrow and shallow, making the climb more difficult. Beatrice kept stubbing her toes on the backs of the stairs and nearly tripping. It became worse when they entered the darkness. Beatrice began to think about vampire bats. She imagined that she could hear the swish of wings around her, but when she stopped to listen, there was only dead silence.

Suddenly a light came on, and everyone gasped.

Quincy held up a flashlight. Its circular beam bounced erratically across the black stone walls.

"You could have warned us," Teddy grumbled.

By the time they reached the top of the stairs, Beatrice and the others were breathing hard.

"How does Grandfather do this?" Quincy demanded between pants. "He's so old."

Teddy giggled, and was about to say something, when the door in front of them slowly began to open.

Against a background of light was the dark silhouette of a small woman in witch's robes. For a moment, no one spoke. Then the woman said softly, "Come in. I've just made a pot of tea."

As they filed into the room, Beatrice looked around with keen interest. She hadn't known exactly what to expect, but she had invisioned something austere and depressing. What a surprise to see how cozy it was!

Winged armchairs were arranged in the center of the room, with a tiny kitchen off to one side. A bank of windows that couldn't be seen from land overlooked the bay. Against that wall, Beatrice saw a narrow bed, shelves crammed with books, and a large telescope. There were bright spots of color everywhere: in the plump chair cushions, the rug on the floor, the pottery that lined the tops of cabinets. And along the windowsills were framed photographs. Beatrice caught sight of Quincy's face grinning at her from inside one of the frames. And there were Xenos and Zara, and Rex and George, and even Miranda. Beatrice glanced at Quincy and saw that he was staring at the photos.

"Please sit down."

Beatrice turned slowly toward the woman. She had been waiting for this moment, and now that it was here, she was overcome with shyness. But as soon as Beatrice looked into Bridget's face, her uneasiness melted away.

It was a small face, softly wrinkled and dominated by gentle brown eyes. Wisps of dark hair just beginning to turn gray had escaped from their clasps and curled at her neck like a child's. She was regarding Beatrice with such a kind expression, it made Beatrice's breath catch in her throat.

They sat down and Bridget poured the tea.

"Thank you for coming," she said. Her tone was as gentle as her eyes, and yet, Beatrice detected a purposeful edge in the woman's voice. She was pretty sure that Bridget had invited them here for a very specific reason.

"Quincy," Bridget said, her gaze coming to rest fondly on him. "The little boy who spied on me."

Quincy grinned and blushed. "You don't know how happy I am to finally meet you, Aunt Bridget," he said quietly.

A smile brushed Bridget's lips, but her eyes were suddenly filled with sadness. "Not as happy as I am to meet you," she murmured. Then she turned to Beatrice. "And I would know you anywhere, Beatrice. I've read about you—every article that's been printed. You're very brave, my dear."

Beatrice could hear only admiration in her voice. There wasn't even a hint of resentment.

"And your friends are brave, as well," Bridget said. "Will you introduce them to me?"

Beatrice complied, and Bridget had a personal comment for each of them. Then Bridget turned to Beatrice, and her brown eyes were bright with intent.

"I can't be away from my duties for long," she said. "I watch the bay through that telescope. When I sight one of the sea monsters approaching the fires, I take action."

"What kind of action?" Beatrice asked.

"I make the fires bigger." Bridget paused and a sigh escaped her lips. "Sometimes that scares them off."

"How do you make the fires bigger, Aunt Bridget?" Quincy asked.

"A blink." Bridget smiled at his blank face. "It's one of my few talents. Two blinks and the fires grow larger, three blinks and they go out." A sorrowful look passed across her face. "I haven't had reason to put them out yet."

"You said that was *one* of your talents," Ollie said.

Bridget smiled sheepishly. "Ah, yes, I can charm snakes, as well. When we were young, Quincy's grandfather and I would go out searching for garter snakes and I found that I could hypnotize them. But I haven't needed *that* talent for a long time."

Bridget turned back to Beatrice, and Beatrice said, "You asked us here for a reason, didn't you?"

Bridget nodded, regardly Beatrice with approval. "You're intuitive. I thought you would be. And yes, my dear, I had a reason for wanting to talk to you—besides being curious, and I'll admit to that also."

Beatrice smiled. She liked this woman very much.

"I've been struggling with something ever since I heard of your arrival in Sea-Dragon Bay," Bridget said. "But perhaps I should tell you a little about my own experience with Dally Rumpe's spell."

Beatrice found herself leaning forward, eager to hear Bridget's story in her own words.

"I was a quiet, timid girl," Bridget said. "I'd never done a courageous thing in my life. Then I learned that I was expected to reverse the spell of a powerful sorcerer." She spread out her hands in dismay. "I had so little talent for magic, and I didn't want to do it, but—one has certain responsibilities in this life. And Xenos—" she glanced at Quincy, "—encouraged me. He always had more faith in me than I had in myself. So I left for Winter Wood."

"Alone?" Beatrice asked quickly.

Bridget nodded.

No wonder she had failed! "I wouldn't have even attempted it without my friends," Beatrice said.

Bridget nodded again, looking around at all of them. "Well, it was too much for me. I didn't even get inside the hedge of thorns. I was terrified." At this, Bridget dropped her eyes. "I was a coward."

"*No!*" they all cried out at once, and Bridget held up a hand to silence them.

"I came home," Bridget said heavily, "and my family tried to comfort me. Xenos felt responsible for encouraging me. And does to this day. Which, of course, is ridiculous," she said stoutly. "*I* was the one who failed. Anyway, everyone expected me to carry on with my life as usual, but that wasn't possible."

The ordeal of remembering, of reliving the most shameful time of her life, had left Bridget pale and drawn.

"You don't have to tell us any more," Beatrice said.

A spark returned to Bridget's eyes. "Oh, but I do," she said. "I have to tell you the most important part. I've had forty years to think about how I would have tried to reach the Island on the Edge—had I made it this far. I still haven't worked it all out, but I might know how to get past the rip currents and out to the sandbar beyond the firedrakes."

Beatrice's heart leaped. "I've been thinking and thinking about the rip currents," she said, "but I haven't had any ideas."

"That's only one of the challenges you must overcome," Bridget said. "There are still the sea monsters and the scorpions and the pirates—"

Beatrice was nodding, too excited to allow her spirits to be dampened. "I understand that, but this is the first piece. We have to take it one step at a time."

"How do we get past the rip currents?" Teddy asked breathlessly.

Bridget was regarding Beatrice closely, a look of indecision on her face. "This is what I've been struggling with. If I tell you, and it doesn't work—"

"But you think it *will* work," Beatrice said.

Bridget was obviously troubled. "I was hoping, instead," she said quietly, "to talk you out of going to Ailsa's island."

Beatrice hadn't expected this. She sat back, stunned.

"I know you have your heart set on going," Bridget said, "but you've already done so much. And it's dangerous." Bridget was picking nervously at the skirt of her robes. "You have no idea, Beatrice. You don't know these waters as I do."

"That's true," Beatrice admitted, "and I know you're doing what you think is best for us. But I can't quit now. You see, I've met two of Bromwich's daughters, Rhona and Innes. I've seen the miserable lives they've had because of Dally Rumpe. And I've promised to try to help their father and their other two sisters. So turning back isn't an option."

Bridget studied Beatrice's face for a long moment. Finally, she said, "I want you to think carefully about the dangers. And I'll think about whether I should help you. We'll meet again soon."

Beatrice started to protest. She wanted to persuade Bridget to tell them *now*. But Bridget's face had closed up. And Beatrice realized that the quiet, timid girl had grown into a woman with a mind of her own.

11

Witch Fever

Quincy opened the door to the castle and peered inside.

"All clear," he whispered.

They came in quietly, intending to hurry up to their rooms before anyone saw them. But they hadn't counted on Miranda.

She was leaning over the railing at the top of the stairs, as if she had been waiting for them. "Where have you been?" she demanded.

"Out," Quincy said, his tone implying that it was none of her business.

Miranda hurried down the stairs, looking furious. "You're helping them, aren't you?" she said to Quincy. "I can't believe you'd take their side against me."

Quincy frowned. "There *are* no sides," he said impatiently. "This is Beatrice's test, Miranda, not yours."

"Who says?" Miranda flared. She was about to say more, but as her eyes drifted over their faces, they stopped abruptly on Teddy's, and her mouth fell open. Suddenly she began to laugh.

Beatrice, Ollie, and Quincy looked at Miranda in bewilderment, then followed her gaze to Teddy's face.

136

"Oh, my gosh," Beatrice said under her breath.

Teddy saw Beatrice's shocked expression and looked frightened. *"What?"* Teddy demanded. Her hand flew up to her face and she touched it gingerly. "Something's wrong . . ." she said uncertainly, and ran over to the hall mirror.

When Teddy saw her reflection, she gasped in horror. The others just stood there in stunned silence. They didn't know what to say.

If it hadn't been for Teddy's curly hair and wire-rim glasses, Beatrice wouldn't have even recognized her friend. Because Teddy's face had turned a bright daffodil yellow, and there were fiery red spots all over her cheeks and forehead. And her nose! Teddy's once pretty little nose was so swollen and misshapen it looked like a big glob of yellow wax stuck to her face.

"This can't be happening," Teddy whispered, and then she screamed.

The sound was enough to send chills down Beatrice's spine, and more than enough to bring Zara, Cyrus, and Sasha from the kitchen, where they had been enjoying a late snack.

"What's wrong?" Zara asked breathlessly. Then she saw Teddy's face, and she just stared.

"Teddy?" Cyrus's eyes bugged out. "Is that—makeup?"

"Makeup? That's right!" Teddy answered hysterically. "It's the latest look. What all the monsters are wearing this season!"

Sasha came over and stared helplessly at Teddy. She tried patting Teddy's arm to comfort her, but Teddy jerked away and covered her face with her hands. Then she began to sob.

"Teddy, you have witch fever," Sasha said. "I did a story on it once, and you look just like the pictures we used for the article."

"She's right," Zara said, embracing a wailing Teddy and resting her chin on Teddy's tumbled curls. "But you won't feel sick, and it only lasts for forty-eight hours."

"Forty-eight hours!" Teddy screeched, and cried harder.

"But she was fine when we left—" Beatrice caught herself. "She was fine a few minutes ago."

"It comes on quickly," Sasha said with authority. "And leaves just as suddenly. But Zara's right—the fever lasts exactly forty-eight hours."

Teddy lifted her yellow face, looking worse than ever now that her eyes were red and swollen from crying. She rubbed her huge nose and hiccuped. "But I don't understand this. I thought that awful medicine was supposed to keep me from getting it."

"I don't understand either," Zara admitted. "Fever Reliever is 100 percent effective."

Beatrice and Ollie exchanged a look.

"Magic," he whispered.

"Sabotage," Beatrice added.

"We'll call Dr. Cattermole," Zara said.

Teddy wiped away tears. "Can he cure it?"

"No, dear," Zara replied. "There's no cure. Unless you were to leave the Witches' Sphere," she added. "Then it would go away automatically."

Teddy's chin began to quiver. *"Nothing's* gone right on this trip, and I've had enough. I don't intend to look like this a second longer than I have to. I'm going home!"

Beatrice couldn't believe she was hearing this. On their other trips to the Sphere, Beatrice, Ollie, and Cyrus had all questioned at one time or another whether they should give up and go home. But not Teddy! She was determined to stay no matter *what* she had to go through.

"Teddy, I know you're upset," Beatrice started.

"You're darn right I'm upset," Teddy cut in, and then she began to cry again. "You'd be upset, too, if you looked like a giant squash."

At this, Miranda began to giggle. Beatrice and Sasha shot her angry looks.

"But don't you see, Teddy?" Beatrice demanded. "Going home is exactly what *someone* wants you to do. Someone who knows that you're especially—" Beatrice searched frantically for a word to replace vain, "—especially *sensitive* about your looks. Are you going to let him—or her—win? You can last forty-eight hours, can't you?"

Teddy was sniffling and mopping her face, but she appeared to be listening.

"And just think," Miranda said suddenly, "with that bright face, you won't need a night-light!" And she bent over in a fit of laughter.

Teddy spun around and glared at Miranda. Beatrice was forced to admit that Teddy's face literally glowed.

"I think you're right, Beatrice," Teddy said tightly. "I won't give *someone* the satisfaction of making me run home. I'm going to stay all right, and *whoever* is responsible for this is going to be sorry."

Beatrice smiled. "I'm proud of you, Teddy," she said. "And I promise, we're going to find out who's been doing all this to us."

"And make them pay," Cyrus said stoutly.

Beatrice was watching Miranda out of the corner of her eye, but the girl didn't look worried. She was still shaking with silent laughter.

＊

Teddy refused to go downstairs for breakfast the next morning and Zara sent up a tray to her room.

"Are you going to stay in this room for forty-eight hours?" Beatrice asked.

"I most certainly am," Teddy replied. "And cover that mirror on your way out, would you?"

Everyone else was already eating when Beatrice and Cayenne entered the dining room. As Beatrice sat down, Miranda gave her an inquiring look.

"How is Teddy this morning?" Miranda asked solicitously. Then she added with a giggle, "Bright *faced* and bushy tailed, I hope."

"That's enough, Miranda," Zara snapped.

While everyone else had wood-tick waffles smothered in sweet violet syrup, Cyrus was chowing down on plain old oatmeal with honey.

"How's your ankle?" Beatrice asked.

"Good as new," Cyrus replied cheerfully.

"But now Teddy's out of commission," Quincy said. He glanced at his watch. "For another thirty-eight hours. I'll go up and see her after breakfast."

"Not a good idea," Beatrice said. "She's pretty embarrassed about how she looks." But Beatrice liked Quincy even more for not *caring* how Teddy looked.

Beatrice noticed that Peregrine still wasn't eating much. He was starting to look haggard.

"Peregrine," she said suddenly, "you need to get out and see the town. Why don't we go to The Firedrake Inn for lunch?"

The witch adviser flashed her one of his crooked smiles, but it seemed to take a lot of effort. "Maybe tomorrow," he said quietly. "I promised to help Angel with his cataloging today."

"Where *is* Angel?" Ollie asked. "Now that he's been kicked out of the library."

"He's working in my study," Xenos said. He sounded annoyed. "I don't know why that investigator had to take over the entire dungeon."

"I hope he didn't have any rat visitors during the night," Beatrice said, her eyes twinkling.

"They'd take one look at him and *run*," Sasha declared.

As if their conversation had summoned him, Junius Sternbuckle suddenly appeared at the dining-room door.

Zara saw him and looked startled. "Er—Mr. Sternbuckle. Won't you join us for breakfast?"

"I ate at seven," the man said, appearing especially somber and self-important. "And then I did some investigative work."

Junius Sternbuckle gave Peregrine a severe look and the witch adviser's left eye began to twitch. "I searched your room," the investigator said, "and found something very interesting."

Xenos's face darkened. "We aren't accustomed to having our guests' rooms searched," he said gruffly.

"I have the authority to search anywhere I choose," Junius Sternbuckle informed him. "And it's a good thing, too, considering what I found." He held up a small leather pouch and said triumphantly, "Twenty gold coins hidden under his mattress."

Peregrine sighed, then lay his head down on the table and didn't move.

Junius Sternbuckle nodded in satisfaction. "He isn't even trying to defend himself. Of course, there is no defense. I've caught you, Peregrine, with more money than you could ever save on your salary. The only way you could have gotten this gold is for Dally Rumpe to have given it to you."

Beatrice and Ollie both started to protest, but Xenos spoke over them. "Wait a minute," he said. "Let me see that gold."

Junius Sternbuckle seemed reluctant to let go of the pouch, but he handed it over grudgingly.

"Hmmm," Xenos said as he turned the pouch over and peered at it. "I thought so," he said. "This is my pouch and my gold. See these initials embossed on the leather? XB— for Xenos Bailiwick."

The investigator looked stunned. "You mean Peregrine stole this pouch from you?"

"I *mean*," Xenos said, "that *someone* took this pouch from my desk. I normally don't keep this much gold around the house, but I haven't made it to the bank this week."

Junius Sternbuckle gave him an accusing look. "And you didn't have it locked in a safe?"

"I don't have a safe," Xenos said, smiling thinly at the man. "A desk drawer seems to work just fine."

"And where *is* this desk?" the investigator asked sharply.

"Down the hall," Xenos replied, "in my study."

At the word *study*, Beatrice glanced quickly at Ollie and they exchanged a look. Beatrice knew that Ollie was as certain as she that Peregrine hadn't stolen Uncle Xenos's gold. Someone had obviously planted the pouch in his room. Anyone in the house would have had the opportunity to go into the study and get the gold, but who was likely to know that the gold coins were in the desk? Xenos had said that Angel Crump was working in his study. At Xenos's *desk*, no doubt. It would have been easy for Angel to take the gold and hide it under Peregrine's mattress. Angel had made it clear enough that he didn't like having Beatrice and her friends around. But what if Angel had more sinister reasons for trying to damage Peregrine's reputation?

Junius Sternbuckle appeared deflated, but he recovered quickly. "Do you want to press charges against this witch for stealing?" he asked Xenos.

"No," Xenos said firmly, "I do not."

Peregrine raised his head and gave Xenos a grateful look. Beatrice, Ollie, and Cyrus beamed at her great-uncle.

The investigator's face contorted with anger. "Out of some misguided loyalty to these—" He stared hard at Beatrice and her friends, "—these—Reform witches?"

Now Xenos looked angry. "I don't have anything else to say," he replied curtly. "It's *my* gold, found in *my* house. I don't believe it's any of your business, Mr. Sternbuckle."

"Let's get out of here," Beatrice said as they were leaving breakfast. "I need some fresh air."

"Good idea," Quincy agreed.

"Can you believe that investigator?" Cyrus demanded, after they had left the castle. "Do you think he's so determined to find Peregrine guilty he could have planted the gold himself?"

"I'm leaning toward Angel," Ollie said. "Quincy, don't you think he probably knows your grandfather's habits better than anyone?"

"*Everyone* knows that Grandfather keeps money in the desk," Quincy replied. "He's always done it. But Angel had the perfect opportunity to get the gold out of the desk. It would have been risky for anyone else to try to sneak into Grandfather's study."

They were walking along the beach in the direction of the tower. Cayenne was pouncing on sand crabs as they darted into their holes.

"Cyrus, how's your ankle doing on the sand?" Beatrice asked.

"It doesn't hurt at all," Cyrus answered. Then he noticed a witch up ahead. "Is that Wadsworth Fretwell?" Cyrus asked.

It was, indeed, Wadsworth Fretwell. He was squatting at the edge of the water holding a sand pail.

Quincy called out a greeting to Wadsworth. "Are you building a sand castle?" Quincy asked cheerfully. "Maybe you should move back a little so the tide won't get it."

Wadsworth Fretwell stood up awkwardly, looking startled. Then he appeared to consider Quincy's comment seriously. "Oh, no. I'm not building anything. These starfish washed up on the beach. They'll die without water. So I'm throwing them back."

"Another good deed," Quincy murmured.

"Well," Wadsworth answered, "I try to be helpful."

They continued down the beach. Beatrice was watching the window in the tower, doubting that she would see Bridget there in broad daylight, but still hoping.

Then she saw movement at the glass. After glancing around to make sure no one was looking, Beatrice waved. Bridget waved back. In a moment, a large piece of paper appeared in the window. Beatrice saw three words printed on it:

COME SEE ME

"Bridget wants to see us," Beatrice said, and they took off for the tower.

Before opening the door, Beatrice looked around again and didn't see anyone. Wadsworth Fretwell had wandered down the beach and had his back to them.

"Are you sure you can make it?" Ollie asked Cyrus as they started up the stairs.

"Just try and stop me!" Cyrus exclaimed. "You guys have had all the fun."

"Right," Beatrice said as they climbed. "Locked in a cellar and nearly drowned, chased by vicious rats, exposed to witch fever. I don't know *when* we've had so much fun."

When they reached the top, Bridget was waiting for them with the door open. Beatrice introduced Cyrus, and Bridget invited them in.

When they were all sitting down, Bridget turned her brown eyes on Beatrice. She didn't waste time with small talk. "Have you thought about what we discussed?" Bridget asked.

"We have," Beatrice said, "and we're going ahead."

Bridget nodded, as if she had been expecting this. "Well, I've been thinking, too," she said. "And I've decided to tell you how *I* would begin the trip to Ailsa's island. But the method hasn't been tested and may not work," she warned them. "There's no way to know for sure until someone tries it."

"We understand," Beatrice said eagerly. "So how do we start?"

"The first step is to get beyond the rip currents that flow from the safe area to the firedrake islands," Bridget said. "I've read about firedrakes in some of Xenos's manuscripts. They tell how the eye of the dragon can be used as a gateway, an astral passageway, if you will."

Seeing their puzzled faces, Bridget explained. "The great Magicians of old believed that dragons were sacred, and the sacred time of the dragon was dawn. They wrote that those of strength and courage could approach the firedrake at dawn, focus on the features of the dragon until the eye is seen, and physically move through the dragon's eye. In one of the manuscripts, I read that you can travel over water this way, but not land. If that's true, you should be able to stand on the beach and visualize your way through the dragon's eye and across the water to the sandbar that lies beyond the fires."

Bridget leaned back in her chair and sighed. "That would get you past the rip currents and some of the deadly sea creatures, but there's still water beyond the sandbar. Water filled with sea monsters, I might add. And other horrors await if you're able to make it to the Island on the Edge. I can't help you with those."

"Could you teach us how to travel through the dragon's eye?" Beatrice asked her.

Bridget studied Beatrice's face. "It's nothing we can practice," she said finally. "If it works, you'll find yourself out on that sandbar with no way to get back." After a moment's hesitation, Bridget added, "But when you're ready to leave for the island, I can meet you on the beach and help you visualize."

Beatrice heard the reluctance in Bridget's voice and thought she understood the reasons for it. Bridget hadn't left this tower in forty years, and now she was promising to meet them outside. What a terrifying prospect *that* must be. And then, what if her plan didn't work? She could be placing Beatrice and her friends in terrible danger.

Beatrice reached for Bridget's hand and squeezed it. "Thank you," she said.

Bridget shook her head to brush aside any gratitude. "I don't know if I'm doing the right thing," she said softly. "This could be an awful mistake. Worse than the one I made forty years ago."

12

Fireworks

By the next morning, Teddy looked worse. Her face was an even brighter yellow, and her nose had puffed out so much it resembled a cabbage. Sasha offered to see what she could do with makeup, and Teddy just stared at her.

"You think makeup will hide *this* schnoz?" she demanded irritably. "Anyway, it should all be gone by tonight. It had *better* be gone."

Beatrice had arranged to meet Ollie, Cyrus, and Quincy in the courtyard after breakfast to begin planning their trip to the Island on the Edge. Ollie had suggested that they draw a diagram of the bay and mark the obstacles they would face at each point. Then they could think about how they were going to overcome the challenges one at a time. Beatrice grabbed paper and felt-tip pens from her backpack, and she and Cayenne started down the stairs.

Quincy, Ollie, and Cyrus were waiting in the front hall. Beatrice could tell from their grim expressions that something was wrong.

"I just heard Sternbuckle talking to Xenos," Ollie said, before she could ask. "He's found more evidence against Peregrine. Someone has been making deposits into

Peregrine's bank account. Just a few dollars here and there, but it's been done regularly for the last two months."

"Sternbuckle thinks the money came from Dally Rumpe," Quincy added.

"This is ridiculous!" Beatrice exploded. "Where's Peregrine now?"

"Grandfather asked him to help Angel catalogue manuscripts this morning," Quincy said. "To keep his mind off things, I imagine."

"What are we going to do?" Cyrus asked. "We aren't helping Peregrine at all."

"Maybe the best way to help him," Ollie said, "is to work on reversing Dally Rumpe's spell. I can't help but believe that Dally Rumpe is behind all the trouble we've had—including Peregrine's problems—so if we break the spell, the case against Peregrine will probably fall apart."

"Let's go outside where no one can hear us and get started," Quincy suggested.

They hurried out to the courtyard and sat down around a stone table to work.

Blowing her bangs aside, Beatrice said, "You're the best artist, Ollie, so you draw."

"Okay," Ollie said, "I'll sketch the castle and the tower first." He picked up a pen and set to work.

"Now put in the firedrakes," Beatrice said. "Five of them straight out from the tower."

"And the sandbar beyond the fires," Cyrus added, pointing to Ollie's drawing. "They should go about here."

Ollie kept drawing.

"Ailsa's island should be on the horizon," Quincy said. "There's a ring of sand around the island, then a narrow strip of water like a moat that has to be crossed."

When Ollie had completed the drawing, he held it up for them to see.

"It looks great," Beatrice said. "Now we need to mark where all the dangers are. Quincy, can you show us where the rip currents start?"

They were just finishing up when Beatrice noticed that Miranda was standing at the front door watching them.

"There's our cousin," Beatrice said, poking Quincy gently with her elbow. "I wonder why she isn't tearing over here to see what we're doing."

In a moment, Beatrice had her answer. Xenos came marching out the front door and headed straight for them, looking really mad. Miranda was right behind him.

Beatrice took one look at the sly smile on Miranda's face and knew that she was up to no good.

Xenos came over to the table, his eyes blazing. "You've been to see Bridget," he barked without preamble. "Against my orders."

Beatrice cut her eyes at Miranda and saw the delighted sparkle in the girl's eyes. So Miranda had ratted on them. That didn't surprise Beatrice a bit.

"How could you be so selfish?" Xenos demanded. "And youth is no excuse. You're old enough to think of other people's needs once in a while."

Miranda was standing slightly behind Xenos, playing at her own version of charades. Her expression changed swiftly as Xenos spoke, first reflecting righteous indignation, then sadness—and finally something real, when her face broke into a grin. *She thinks this is all a joke*, Beatrice thought, and wanted to belt her.

"My sister has been through more misery than you could ever imagine," Xenos went on, his voice growing louder and louder. "Where is your compassion? Your understanding?"

Now Zara and Ulysses were coming out of the castle to see what was going on. Then Sasha, already digging into her pocket for notebook and pen.

"Papa," Ulysses said in a stage whisper, "everyone in town can hear you."

This seemed to incense Xenos even more. "Do I look like I care?" he demanded, and started in on Beatrice and the others again.

"But Papa Bailiwick," Zara interrupted him, "I'm sure they didn't mean any harm."

"I'm not concerned with their intent," Xenos snapped. "They disobeyed me."

Ulysses was frowning at his wife. "They disobeyed him," Ulysses repeated.

Zara shot Ulysses an irritated look. "Are you your father's parrot now?"

"Ulysses, I don't need your help!" Xenos bellowed.

And then it seemed to Beatrice that the adults had forgotten about Bridget altogether as they started yelling at each other. Zara was standing with her hands on her hips and her head thrown back shouting at Ulysses, and Ulysses was shaking his finger at Zara and screaming over her voice. And Xenos was yelling at both of them.

Beatrice glanced anxiously at Quincy, who appeared unconcerned.

"Don't let it upset you," Quincy said loudly, in order to be heard over his parents and grandfather. "They do this all the time. Doesn't mean a thing."

Suddenly there was a small explosion overhead. Then another. Beatrice, Ollie, and Cyrus looked up, and were surprised to see skyrockets shooting through the clouds. Before long, the entire sky above The Sandcastle was lit up with bursts of pink and blue and green fireworks. It was beautiful!

Xenos, Zara, and Ulysses had stopped shouting and were staring at the sky, as well. The fireworks seemed to have had a calming effect because they were even smiling a little.

Quincy grinned at Beatrice. "This is how all their fights end," he said. "They make the best fireworks in Sea-Dragon Bay."

When everything had quieted down, Beatrice said, "Uncle Xenos, may I say something?"

Xenos's temper was spent. He nodded, appearing more tired than angry.

"It's just that Bridget wants to help us," Beatrice said. "Maybe I don't know her well enough to say this, but I think by helping us, she could also help herself. Anyway, she's an adult, isn't she? Shouldn't she be able to decide who she will and won't see?"

Xenos stared at Beatrice for what seemed an eternity, his brows knit together like he might start yelling again. But then he nodded and said, "What you say is true, Beatrice. Whether I like it or not. I don't want my sister to be hurt again, but if she's willing to take the risk, who am I to stand in her way?"

"We need some fun," Quincy said after the adults and Miranda had gone back inside. "Why don't I take you to The Firedrake Inn for lunch?"

"Every time we plan to go, something happens," Beatrice remarked.

And this time was no exception. They were just about to leave the courtyard when a uniformed Ghost Guard officer came through the gate with Rex, George, and Kolliwobbles in tow. The boys and the pixie looked scared to death, so Beatrice knew they were in trouble.

The ghost knocked on the wide double doors and Xenos himself answered the summons. Beatrice, Ollie, Cyrus, and Quincy came forward shamelessly to listen.

Xenos glanced at the nanny's woebegone face and sighed. "What is it this time?" he asked.

"I found them down at the pier," the officer said. "A small sea serpent had slipped past the bonfires and made its way to shore." The ghost frowned. "And these three were feeding it jelly beans. Someone should tell them that sea serpents aren't pets!"

Kolliwobbles lifted his glum face to Xenos. "It was a very *little* sea serpent," he mumbled.

Xenos's jaw tightened. "Thank you, officer," he said. "I can assure you that my grandsons will never be any trouble to you again."

"Good day to you, sir," the ghost said, and turned to leave.

Xenos was looking down at the boys and their nanny. "Rex, you and George won't be leaving the house for a while," he said firmly. "As a matter of fact, you'll be staying inside until you prove to me that I can trust you. Now go up to your room."

The boys didn't need to be told twice and shot through the door.

"What about me?" Kolliwobbles asked in a small voice. "Am I confined to the house with Rex and George?"

Beatrice expected her great-uncle to give the pixie a stern lecture, but Xenos just looked at Kolliwobbles with a sad expression on his face.

The pixie blinked and shifted nervously. "I did wrong," he said. "It won't happen again."

"No, Kolliwobbles, it won't," Xenos said. His voice was surprisingly gentle. "I've given you every chance to show that you can be a responsible nanny for my grandsons. But I can't trust you with them—not after this. Rex and George could have been badly hurt. Or worse."

Kolliwobbles was looking scared, and Beatrice found herself feeling sorry for him. Even though she knew her great-uncle was right. What nanny in his right mind would allow little boys to play with a *sea serpent?*

"I'm going to have to let you go," Xenos said quietly. "You'll get two months' severance pay, and I'm sure you'll find another position by that time."

"I'll do better," the pixie said quickly. "No more sea serpents. I promise."

"You've made too many promises and haven't kept any of them," Xenos said. "I'm sorry."

Kolliwobbles's chin jerked up and his mouth tightened as he looked at Xenos. "You *will* be sorry," he muttered. "*Very* sorry." The pixie's innocent baby face was suddenly transformed by anger. Someone hard and spiteful was staring out through those narrowed blue eyes.

Xenos's expression froze. "You'd better leave," he said coldly.

"I'll leave, all right!" Kolliwobbles shouted. "But you haven't seen the last of me. Do you hear that, you mean old witch? You'll wish you'd treated me better!"

The Firedrake Inn was large and rambling, turned silver-gray by the sun and salt air. It rode the tops of the dunes like a great seabird.

Quincy crossed the wide shaded veranda and led them inside. The lobby, which should have been filled with vacationers, was empty and hauntingly silent. Not so with the dining room. The older man who led them to a table overlooking the water said to Quincy, "I hope the singing doesn't bother you. They can get pretty rowdy at times, but they're our only regular customers."

"No, Rudo," Quincy said. "I'm glad to see the business."

Beatrice sat down and placed Cayenne in the chair beside her. They both looked with interest to the other side of the room where a half-dozen pirates were raising mugs and singing a sea chanty at the tops of their lungs. Actually, they were ghost pirates, Beatrice realized, noticing their wispy edges.

"Is that Blackbeard?" Ollie asked. He was staring in fascination at a tall pirate in a fancy red coat, his long black beard braided into a dozen tails and tied with red ribbons.

"It is," Quincy said. "And luckily for us, he's a big spender. A waitress can expect a gold piece or two before he leaves. That's Calico Jack leading the singing. And the woman is Anne Bonny."

"She was a pirate, too?" Beatrice asked, looking at the hard-faced woman who was dressed in men's breeches and waving a sword over her head as she sang.

"One of the most bloodthirsty to ever sail the seas," Quincy answered with a grin. "They say that during their pirating days even Blackbeard stayed out of her way."

Ollie was surveying the menu with pleasure. "I love seafood. Shrimp and locusts sounds good. Or maybe I'll have the flounder and earthworms."

Beatrice was still watching the pirates. Then she saw a familiar face among them. It was Wadsworth Fretwell, waving a mug in the air and humming along with the singing.

"What's *he* doing with them?" Beatrice asked.

Quincy glanced up from his menu. "Oh, you mean Wadsworth? Blackbeard has sort of made a pet of him. It's sad, really. Wadsworth thinks they're his friends, but I don't think Blackbeard would give him the time of day except for the Dally Rumpe connection."

Beatrice's eyes darted to Quincy's face. "What do you mean?" she asked. "*What* Dally Rumpe connection?"

Quincy looked surprised. "You don't know? I just assumed that you would. Well—I guess I'd better tell you, Beatrice. Wadsworth Fretwell is Dally Rumpe's only known living descendent."

13

Family Likeness

"He could be working for Dally Rumpe!" Beatrice exclaimed.

"I guess," Quincy replied, but he didn't sound convinced. "The truth is, I've always felt sorry for Wadsworth. Witches in town don't have much to do with him because of his family history, and he just seems sad to me. And all these pathetic good deeds he does? I think he's trying to show people that he's nothing like Dally Rumpe."

The pirates had finished their meal and were fading out of the room, leaving Wadsworth alone at the table. He was still waving his mug and humming—then a startled look crossed his face as he noticed that the pirates were gone. He set the mug down heavily, appearing depressed.

"I'm going over to talk to him," Beatrice said.

"You can't just come out and ask him if he's working for Dally Rumpe," Ollie said. "Or expect an honest answer from him, anyway."

"No," Beatrice agreed. "But when I mention Dally Rumpe, maybe I'll catch him off guard and he'll reveal something."

Wadsworth's gloom lifted when he saw Beatrice approaching the table. He smiled and scratched his neck. "Good afternoon," he said as he leaped up from the table—and knocked over his mug.

"Sit down, please," Beatrice said hastily. "I was wondering if I could talk to you for a minute."

"Certainly," Wadsworth replied, rubbing his hands together nervously.

Beatrice sat down across from him. She considered starting out with some innocent chitchat, and then decided to just spring it on him. "I understand that you're related to the sorcerer Dally Rumpe," Beatrice said, her eyes glued to his face.

Wadsworth Fretwell's mouth fell open and he blinked rapidly several times. "Yes, that's true," he answered. "I hope you won't hold it against me. A witch can't choose his family, after all."

Watching him, Beatrice decided that he didn't look especially guilty, but she had definitely taken him by surprise. "Then you aren't working for Dally Rumpe?" she asked bluntly.

Wadsworth gulped so hard his Adam's apple started to vibrate. "*Me?*" he asked, plainly startled and dismayed. "Why, no. *Absolutely not!* I'm a *good* witch. I try to be helpful. I try to have compassion. I try—"

"Of course you do," Beatrice said quickly. *Either he's innocent,* Beatrice thought, *or an excellent actor.* But then she knew from her encounters with Dally Rumpe that a talent for acting seemed to run in the family.

"I would *never* get involved in such nasty business," Wadsworth said vehemently. "That's why I'm not mad at you. Like the rest of the town. I *want* you to break his spell." Wadsworth appeared sincere when he added, "I might even be able to help you."

"Really?" Beatrice thought it best to stay noncommittal and just let him talk.

There was a glint in the depths of his black eyes and he leaned forward slightly, betraying his excitement. "You see," he said, lowering his voice to a confidential whisper, "I've been researching Dally Rumpe's life for years, and I've written a book about him. It contains things that very few people know. I could show it to you," he said eagerly.

The man's sallow face was only inches from Beatrice's own. He had large oily pores and prickly stubble on his chin. And he didn't appear especially clean. She had conflicting emotions about Wadsworth, ranging from revulsion to pity.

"It would help you to understand Dally Rumpe better," Wadsworth added.

The man appeared earnest, but Beatrice picked up on a sly undercurrent in his voice. Her instincts told her that—pathetic or not—Wadsworth Fretwell was devious. But the book tempted her. She wanted to learn everything she could about her adversary.

Beatrice found herself saying, "I'd like to see your book very much. May I borrow it?"

Wadsworth nodded, his eyes glittering. "I always keep it with me," he said softly.

Reaching into a large canvas bag he carried over his shoulder, Wadsworth withdrew a thick manuscript covered with a homemade cardboard binding. Across the front, Wadsworth had scrawled the title in black ink. *Dally Rumpe: The Life of a Sorcerer Gone Bad.*

Wadsworth looked down at the manuscript and then back at Beatrice, his brows drawn together in a frown. "This is my life's work," he said. "You must take very good care of it."

"I will," Beatrice said, reaching for the manuscript. "I promise."

"And one more thing," he said, burrowing into his bag again. "I can't let you have this, but you can look at it." He withdrew a small oil painting and held it out for her to see.

It was a portrait of a man in black witch's robes. He was tall and thin, with a narrow aristocratic face and short black hair. *Handsome*, Beatrice thought. And also vaguely familiar.

Beatrice glanced up at Wadsworth. "This is Dally Rumpe?" she asked.

He nodded, not lifting his eyes from the portrait.

"I thought he would be more . . ."

"Beastly?" Wadsworth suggested, and Beatrice saw the sly glint in his eyes again.

"He revealed himself to me in Werewolf Close," Beatrice said, "and he was horrible."

"He showed you what he's become," Wadsworth said, then nodded at the painting. "This is what he *was*. As a young man. Before all the evil doings started."

"He looks like someone," Beatrice mused.

And then it came to her. She knew *exactly* who Dally Rumpe looked like. "Miranda!" Beatrice said in astonishment. "My cousin," she added absently to Wadsworth.

"I know who she is," he answered. "I saw the resemblance myself. And why not?" he asked, a faint smile forming on his lips. "After all, they're related."

Beatrice's head shot up. "What are you talking about?"

Wadsworth Fretwell was pleased with himself. He was grinning and seemed barely able to contain his mirth. "I don't want to ruin it for you," he said blithely. "Read my book, Beatrice Bailiwick, and you'll see. You'll see it all."

Beatrice didn't talk to anyone about her conversation with Wadsworth. It was an impulsive decision, based on an uneasy feeling that she needed to read the manuscript first. They all noticed the dog-eared volume when she brought it back to the table, and amidst their other questions, Ollie asked about the manuscript. Beatrice just said that Wadsworth fancied himself a writer and wanted her to look at his work. She knew that really bad poetry and short stories would come to mind—and sure enough, everyone at the table grinned and gave her pitying looks.

Beatrice wanted to start reading the manuscript as soon as they got home, but a yellow-faced Teddy was still holed up in their room, and Beatrice needed privacy. She was wandering the halls of the castle looking for a place to hide out when something happened that made her forget all about the manuscript.

Beatrice was walking down a back corridor when she heard whispered voices in the kitchen. Peeking inside, she saw Miranda standing with the outside door open. Her cousin was talking to someone, and there was an intensity in Miranda's tone that caught Beatrice's attention. She crept into the room to listen.

Someone was saying, "I did good, didn't I?"

Beatrice recognized that voice. She peered around the refrigerator, and sure enough, there was Kolliwobbles grinning up at Miranda.

"So far," Miranda said grudgingly.

"Then where's my money?" the pixie demanded.

As Beatrice watched, Miranda pulled a roll of bills from her pocket and handed it to him.

Kolliwobbles counted it quickly. Then he scowled. "This is only half what you promised."

"You'll get the other half when we're finished," Miranda said curtly.

"But—"

"If you argue with me, you may not get the rest at all," Miranda snapped. "I'll be in touch."

Miranda closed the door swiftly. Before she could turn around, Beatrice slipped out of the kitchen and hurried down the corridor. She was still glancing nervously over her shoulder when she ran into Ollie and Cyrus in the front hall.

"Come outside," Beatrice said.

"What's going on?" Ollie asked as he and Cyrus followed Beatrice into the courtyard.

Beatrice quickly told them about seeing Miranda and Kolliwobbles.

"So she's paying him to do something for her," Ollie said.

"And being very secretive about it," Beatrice answered. She nearly told them about the portrait she had seen of Dally Rumpe, and how much Miranda looked like the evil sorcerer. But how did she know that

162

Wadsworth was telling the truth about Miranda being related to Dally Rumpe? That painting could be a portrait of anyone.

Just then, the front door swung open. Quincy stuck his head out and motioned for them to come. "There's more trouble," Quincy said. "You'd better get in here."

"Grandfather's study," Quincy said when they were inside, and started down the corridor.

The door to the study was open, and they could see Xenos and Junius Sternbuckle standing near the door. Angel was sitting behind Xenos's massive desk staring up at the two men. Then Beatrice noticed Peregrine, who was nearly hidden behind a tall stack of manuscripts.

"I don't believe it," Xenos was saying. "If a strange witch had been in my home, I would have known it."

The investigator's face hardened. "I'm telling you, I have an eyewitness. Someone saw Peregrine meeting with this stranger in the middle of the night. And taking money from him!"

Xenos's expression had turned stubborn. "No one in my family would have reported something like that to you without telling me first."

Junius Sternbuckle raised his eyebrows. "Did I say it was a member of your family?"

"Who else would have been in my home late at night?" Xenos demanded. "You'd better tell me right now who made these allegations."

The investigator's lips twisted into a parody of a smile. "It was your nanny," he said in quiet triumph.

"*Kolliwobbles?*" Xenos looked shocked, then disgusted. "He's hardly a reliable witness. I just fired that pixie, and he didn't take it well. He would say anything to cause trouble."

Junius Sternbuckle glared at Xenos. "He appeared reliable enough to me. And I intend to include his testimony in my report."

Beatrice saw Peregrine's shoulders sag. Then he let out a long sigh.

"Do what you have to," Xenos said gruffly. "I think I'll be hiring an investigator of my own to get to the bottom of this. Forgive me, Mr. Sternbuckle, but it doesn't seem to me that you've been exactly impartial."

Beatrice, Ollie, Cyrus, and Quincy didn't wait to hear the heated accusations and denials that followed. They went back outside to talk.

Beatrice was furious. "We were right about Miranda all along!" she sputtered. "She paid Kolliwobbles to lie about seeing Peregrine taking money from a stranger."

Quincy's head jerked up. "What are you talking about?"

Beatrice told him about overhearing Miranda and Kolliwobbles.

Quincy's eyes grew larger as he listened. "I can't believe it," he muttered. "I knew Miranda was greedy and self-centered, but I never imagined she could do something so—"

"Evil?" Beatrice finished for him.

"But how do we prove it?" Ollie asked. "Beatrice, it's your word against Miranda's."

"Maybe we can trick her into confessing," Cyrus said.

Quincy was thinking hard. "I have an idea," he said.

14

A Very Bad Witch

Beatrice was waiting outside with Ollie and Cyrus when Quincy returned.

"Did you find Kolliwobbles?" Beatrice asked.

Quincy nodded. "He was down at the video arcade blowing the money Miranda gave him."

"Did he admit that she paid him to lie about Peregrine?" Ollie prompted. "Is he going to help us?"

"Yes and yes." Quincy smiled wryly. "For a price. Luckily, Kolliwobbles's tastes are simple. A year's advance on my allowance should do the trick."

"We'll all chip in," Beatrice assured him. "So when is he coming?"

"In about an hour," Quincy said. "Now we need to find Sasha and see if she'll loan us her digital recorder."

Beatrice frowned. "We'll have to tell her why. And then she'll want to write about it."

Quincy was watching her closely. "You still don't want to betray Miranda," he said gently. "Even though she tried to ruin Peregrine."

Beatrice shrugged. "Silly, isn't it?"

"Family loyalty isn't silly," Quincy replied. "But after Kolliwobbles talks to Miranda, we may find out that she's done even worse things. I rehearsed with him what he's supposed to say."

"Do you think this is going to work?" Beatrice looked worried. "He's so—scatterbrained."

Quincy grinned. "He seemed pretty focused when we started talking money. Plus, he's mad at Miranda. He thinks she's going to cheat him out of the money she owes him."

They found Sasha in the room she shared with Miranda working at her laptop.

"Where's Miranda?" Beatrice asked.

Sasha rolled her eyes. "In the bathroom giving herself a facial. That girl spends more time on beauty regimens than anyone I've ever met."

"Could we talk to you a minute?" Beatrice asked. "Outside?"

Sasha looked surprised. Then she grinned and leaped up from her computer. "Something's going on, isn't it?"

"You have one of those little recorders that slips in a pocket, don't you?" Ollie asked. "Can you bring that with you?"

When Kolliwobbles arrived, Quincy took him to a corner of the courtyard where no one in the castle could see him. After slipping the minuscule recorder into the pixie's shirt pocket, Quincy said, "Stand facing her and not too far away. Now before I go get her, do you remember what we need to know?"

The pixie looked mildly offended. "I think I can manage," he replied stiffly.

Beatrice, Ollie, Cyrus, and Cayenne were hidden nearby behind a tangle of bougainvillea vines. They could see the blue of Kolliwobbles's shorts and the nervous tapping of his skinny foot on the flagstone walk. Then they saw Miranda hurrying from the house toward the pixie.

"What are you doing here?" she hissed. "You know we can't be seen together. What if Quincy tells Grandfather?"

"He won't," Kolliwobbles said. "Quincy likes me. He thinks your grandfather was wrong to fire me."

"So what do you want?" Miranda demanded. "If it's the money—"

"I was just worried," Kolliwobbles said, and he actually sounded worried. "What if they figure out what we did? I've heard Beatrice say she doesn't trust you."

Miranda's laugh was harsh. "Nor should she. But they can't prove a thing."

"She already suspects that you're the one who filed charges against Peregrine."

"But the Witches' Institute has to keep that confidential," Miranda answered smugly. "They aren't allowed to release my name. So stop worrying, no one will ever know you lied to that investigator."

"You really are a very bad witch, Miranda," Kolliwobbles said.

Beatrice could hear the admiration in his voice, and she thought, *This pixie is good!* But she was also feeling a little sick now that she knew for certain that it was Miranda—*her cousin*—who was out to get Peregrine.

Miranda was laughing again, obviously pleased. "You don't know the half of it," she said darkly.

"Why? What else have you done?" Kolliwobbles asked eagerly. "You couldn't have thought up anything worse than the lies about that witch adviser."

"No? What would you say if I told you that I caused the hot-air balloon to crash into the bay?"

"*You* did that? But how?"

"It was easy," Miranda said. "I can cast spells to make things not work. I used the spell on a cord in the balloon so the pilot couldn't close the parachute valve."

Beatrice remembered Quincy teasing Miranda about being able to cast only one spell. And what a handy one for her purposes!

"Then I did some other things," Miranda bragged, "like making the elevator not work properly, and that klutzy Cyrus fell out. And I made doors not work, so Ollie was locked in a cellar at high tide and Beatrice in the dungeon with the rats. I had removed the vent earlier, hoping that I'd have a chance to lock someone in the storeroom, and put cheese inside the vent shaft to attract the rats."

"And you gave Peregrine the gifts and planted Xenos's gold in his room?"

"Of course." Suddenly Miranda laughed. "And the best yet was making Teddy's Fever Reliever not work. I thought Teddy was going to have a breakdown when she saw how hideous she looked!"

Beatrice couldn't believe that Miranda was spilling all her secrets like this. But she had to hand it to Kolliwobbles.

He had managed Miranda just right, playing to her conceit. And Miranda had thrown discretion to the wind now that she had an audience who seemed to appreciate the brilliance of her diabolical deeds.

"What I don't understand," Miranda was saying now, "is why they haven't run out of here in terror. Of course, Quincy and Bridget are helping them," she added petulantly, "and Bridget won't even *see* me! It doesn't make sense," Miranda said, sounding genuinely puzzled. "Why doesn't anyone like me?"

Cyrus, Ollie, and Quincy went with Beatrice to Xenos's study. Beatrice's great-uncle was seated at his desk reading a manuscript that appeared very old and scholarly. Angel and Peregrine were working at a table in the corner.

All three looked up when Beatrice tapped on the door.

"I think you should hear this," Beatrice said, and handed her great-uncle the recorder.

"What is it?" Xenos asked.

"You should probably interpret it for yourself, Grandfather," Quincy said.

Peregrine was looking at Beatrice with quizzical eyes. She winked at him.

Xenos pressed the On button, and Miranda's voice filled the room.

"What are you doing here? You know we can't be seen together . . ."

No one spoke, or so much as blinked, while the recorder played. When it was finished, Xenos reached over slowly to turn it off. Then he raised his eyes to Beatrice. His face was ravaged.

"I can't believe it," Xenos said heavily. "My own granddaughter doing such despicable things!"

Peregrine's face registered shock at first. Then his lips began to lift into a crooked smile.

"Grandfather, this proves that Miranda trumped up the charges against Peregrine," Quincy said quietly.

Xenos nodded woodenly. "Not to mention putting Beatrice and her friends into terrible danger. And herself, as well!" Xenos's eyes blazed. "Didn't she realize that she could have been killed herself when that balloon went down?"

"I think," Beatrice said slowly, searching for tactful words, "that Miranda's ambition was greater than any fear she might have felt. She was so determined to get rid of us and break Dally Rumpe's spell herself, she couldn't let the dangers stop her."

Xenos's eyes were suspiciously bright. "I don't know how a daughter of mine could raise such a child," he muttered. Then he grimaced. "Not that Willow doesn't have a ruthless side. When she was small, I caught her in little lies, but I thought she would outgrow it. I spoiled her, and allowed her to become a person with very little integrity. Now it looks as if Miranda is following in her mother's footsteps."

"But she's very bright," Angel said suddenly. "You have to admire Miranda's intelligence and ingenuity."

Everyone in the room just stared at him.

Angel scowled. "Well, it's true," he mumbled.

"I'm not quite sure how to handle this," Xenos said soberly. "I'll talk to Miranda, of course. And until I decide what to do, she'll be confined to her room. I can't send her home," he went on, more to himself than anyone else. "Willow would just let her run wild. But she'll have to be sent *somewhere*."

Beatrice felt sorry for her great-uncle. He was a good, honest witch, and she knew that it must be a crushing blow to realize that his granddaughter was the exact opposite.

Quincy cleared his throat, looking uncomfortable. "What Miranda did goes beyond childish pranks," Quincy said gently. "This is really a police matter, Grandfather."

Xenos's face became hard. "I'll tell Miranda if she does anything to interfere with Beatrice's plans, or to harm *anyone*, I'll call the police myself. But I have to think about this for a while."

At twenty minutes past nine that night, Teddy's face suddenly became normal again. She had been sitting in front of the mirror for an hour, waiting for it to happen.

As her skin turned from yellow to pink, and the red blotches vanished, and her cabbage nose became small and perky again, Teddy began to cry. "Thank goodness," she blubbered. "I was afraid everyone was wrong and I was going to stay this way forever."

"You look wonderful," Beatrice said kindly, and hugged her friend. "I don't think I ever noticed how really beautiful you are."

Teddy's smile illuminated her entire face, and she started to cry harder.

"You should go see Quincy," Beatrice said. "He's been really worried about you."

Teddy stopped mopping at her wet face. "He has?" she asked brightly. Then she frowned and sniffled. "You know, it's so unfair. First I have to look like a freak for two days, and then I miss Miranda getting caught. What's going to happen to her, anyway? She won't get off scot-free, will she?"

"Grandfather's thinking it over," Beatrice said. While she was relieved that the truth was finally known, Beatrice couldn't hope for revenge like Teddy. "For the time being, she's confined to her room."

Teddy frowned. "*That's* not going to keep her from coming after us. She needs to be locked up!"

After Teddy was asleep, Beatrice crawled into bed beside Cayenne and finally opened the Dally Rumpe manuscript. Wadsworth Fretwell's grammar wasn't the best, but the story he had written about his kinsman captivated Beatrice from the first sentence. Then the narrative took a turn that Beatrice never would have imagined. The words filled her with shock and a growing sense of dread.

Two hours later, Beatrice closed the manuscript. She sat there for a long time, feeling numb, burdened by ancient secrets both sad and horrifying. She would have to ask Xenos about it. But somehow, Beatrice knew that Wadsworth had written the truth.

15

Who Is Dally Rumpe?

When Beatrice and her friends were coming down the stairs for breakfast the next morning, they saw Junius Sternbuckle headed for the door with his briefcase and luggage. His indignant face was the happiest sight Beatrice had seen in days. The investigator glared up at them before slamming the door shut behind him.

Everyone else was already gathered around the dining-room table. Only Miranda was noticeably absent.

Peregrine beamed when he saw Beatrice come in with Cayenne riding on her shoulder. Beatrice beamed back and Cayenne meowed.

"Is it official?" Beatrice asked.

Xenos nodded, looking pleased. "The charges against Peregrine have been dropped. Thanks to you young witches," he added. Then a shadow crossed his face, and Beatrice knew that her great-uncle was thinking about Miranda.

"What a scoop!" Sasha said happily as she scribbled in her notebook.

"But you promised—" Beatrice started.

"No names," Sasha said, momentarily gloomy. Then she perked up. "But no other reporter even knows about the charges. I can still write the story and say that Peregrine was cleared without using Miranda's name."

Peregrine was looking a little weepy. He swallowed hard. "I don't know how to thank you all," he said, sniffling a little as he looked at the smiling faces around him.

"Peregrine, you haven't eaten in days," Zara said. "I'll cook a special dinner tonight."

"That sounds very nice," Peregrine said, "but I've been told to return to the Institute right after breakfast. To resume my duties," he added, giving them all a watery grin.

"You'll be back," Beatrice said quickly.

"As soon as you've broken Dally Rumpe's spell," Peregrine promised.

After breakfast, Beatrice caught up with Xenos as he was leaving the dining room.

"I need to talk with you when you have time," Beatrice said. "It's about something Wadsworth Fretwell gave me to read."

Xenos looked at her steadily. "His biography of Dally Rumpe."

Beatrice was surprised. "You know about it?"

"He let me read it a few months ago."

Beatrice felt her adrenaline begin to pump. "Is what he wrote true?"

Xenos glanced beyond Beatrice at Quincy, Teddy, Ollie, and Cyrus, who had stayed behind to listen. "Why don't you all come into my study? Angel's gone out to run errands, so we'll have some privacy."

Once they were settled in chairs around Xenos's desk, and Cayenne had curled up in the in-box to take a nap, Quincy looked at Beatrice and said, "It was Dally Rumpe's life story that Wadsworth gave you?"

Beatrice nodded. "I wanted to read it before I said anything."

"So now you know," Xenos said.

"Know what?" Quincy asked.

Xenos looked solemnly at his grandson. "That Dally Rumpe is a Bailiwick."

The room froze. Then Beatrice's voice rose from the silence. "So everything Wadsworth wrote is true?"

"It is," Xenos replied. "My father told me about it when I was a young man. I thought I would pass on the information to Quincy when he was older. The Bailiwicks aren't proud of the facts contained in Wadsworth's manuscript, so they've kept quiet about it. Most of our family doesn't even know. But I don't believe the truth should be lost."

Quincy was rubbing his brow, looking stunned. "You mean, we're related to Dally Rumpe?"

"The same as Wadsworth," Xenos replied.

Quincy just shook his head. "I think you'd better start at the beginning on this one."

"That goes back a long time," Xenos said, "almost two hundred and fifty years, to an ancestor named Lazarus Bailiwick. He and his wife Nebula had two sons, Dalbert and Bromwich. Lazarus favored his younger son because Bromwich was smart and personable and magically gifted. Lazarus had very little talent for magic, but he admired sorcerers, so Bromwich's skill with magic was very important to him. Lazarus thought his older son, Dalbert, was lazy and arrogant. Plus," Xenos went on, "Dalbert had a terrible temper that he let loose once too often on his father. As the elder son, Dalbert expected to inherit everything, but Lazarus left the kingdom of Bailiwick to Bromwich. All Dalbert received was an old book of spells. His father enclosed a note advising Dalbert to study the book well— saying that if he could become even half the sorcerer his brother was, he might still make something of himself."

"What a cruel thing to say," Teddy murmured.

"From what I can tell, Lazarus wasn't an especially nice man," Xenos agreed. "Anyway, Dalbert went nearly mad with fury, and from that day on, he refused to use his father's name. He took his mother's maiden name as his own."

"Was her name Rumpe by any chance?" Ollie asked.

Xenos smiled grimly. "You guessed it. Dalbert was always called Dally by his mother, and on the day his father died, Dalbert Bailiwick became Dally Rumpe. He left home and went to live in a remote cave in the mountains. He lived off the land and followed his father's advice—for his own purposes, of course—studying the book of spells for hours on end. During the years that followed, Dally Rumpe made the association of all sorts of disreputable creatures—ghouls and evil imps and the like—who came to view him as their leader."

"I thought Wadsworth was sympathetic to Dally Rumpe in the manuscript," Beatrice said. "He implied that what Dally Rumpe became was his father's fault."

Xenos sighed. "Things might be different today if Lazarus had tried to treat the two boys the same, but it was still Dally Rumpe's decision to turn to evil. No one else can be held responsible."

"So he lived in a cave and studied the book of spells," Cyrus prompted, eager to hear more.

"He learned a great deal about magic," Xenos said, "and discovered that he had more talent than his father had given him credit for. And when he was ready, he went after the kingdom of Bailiwick, which he saw as rightfully his. But he wasn't quite powerful enough, and his spell had unexpected results."

"It split the kingdom into five parts," Beatrice said, "and each became a land of extremes."

"Exactly," Xenos responded. "But I don't think Dally Rumpe even cared about that. By then, he had become a madman, and all he really wanted was to pay his father and Bromwich back for what he saw as their betrayal. He could have killed Bromwich and his daughters, and people have often speculated about why he decided to hold them captive instead. I believe it's because, in the final moment, Dally Rumpe still felt a kinship to Bromwich. Even though he had become a monster, family still meant *something* to him. So he allowed Bromwich and the girls to live—if you can call their circumstances a life."

Beatrice felt suddenly cold. She was just beginning to understand something, at a deep gut level. The blood that ran through Dally Rumpe's veins was *her* blood.

Xenos was looking at her now. His eyes were kind. "I thought about telling you," he said, "but I could see that you're compassionate and caring. I wasn't sure you'd be able to go after a member of your own family."

Beatrice nodded. "You were right, this may make it more—difficult. But Rhona and Innes are my family, too," she said with a rush of feeling, "and I saw with my own eyes how terrible it was for them."

"This is weird," Ollie said suddenly. "History repeating itself. First, Dalbert is jealous of his brother and that makes him do bad things. And now Miranda is jealous of her cousin—"

"And gives me that hideous witch fever!" Teddy burst out indignantly.

"You aren't the only one she hurt," Beatrice said dryly.

Xenos appeared pensive now. "When I first learned that we're related to Dally Rumpe, I realized that the Bailiwicks have the capacity for both good and evil. I'd always hoped that Miranda's selfishness would lessen as she grew older, that she'd become a good person. That's why I was glad when Willow and Ephraim took her to the mortal world, away from magical influences. But obviously, leaving the Sphere hasn't helped."

Beatrice understood how gravely disappointed he was in his granddaughter. But it would be dangerous to keep hoping that Miranda was going to turn around and become someone completely different. They had to face facts: Dally Rumpe and Miranda had more in common than a physical resemblance. *Could they be working together?* Beatrice wondered. *And what about Wadsworth Fretwell? Was it possible that he, as well as Miranda, was supporting Dally Rumpe?*

Then Beatrice's thoughts shifted to another potential problem. "Let's not tell Sasha about Dally Rumpe's relationship to the Bailiwicks. I'm not sure she could resist writing about something this hot."

When they left Xenos's study, a surprise awaited them in the front hall. There they found Rex and George sitting on the back of a giant sea turtle. The creature was incredibly ugly, with a leathery greenish brown head and massive legs covered with wartlike growths. It was about the size of a compact car.

"What's this?" Xenos exclaimed. "Rather large for an indoor pet."

"George saw it out the window," Zara said in exasperation, "and suddenly it was just *here!*"

Xenos raised his eyebrows. Then he smiled. "I think these boys are showing promise," he said softly to Zara. "They may have more talent than all the rest of us put together."

Zara's eyes widened in horror. "What a nightmare," she muttered.

"They just need guidance," Xenos assured her. "We have to find them a nanny who can help them learn to use their talents constructively."

"We've already got a nanny," Rex informed them. He glanced down at the sea turtle and patted the creature's hard shell. "Meet Horatio."

"You can't have a sea turtle for a nanny," Zara said impatiently.

"Why not?" George demanded. "That's why I brought him here. And he likes the idea."

Thinking fast, Zara answered, "Because he needs to be in the water. And because he—he has to be able to speak."

At that, Horatio turned his great wrinkled head toward Zara and blinked. "Actually," the sea turtle said calmly, "I *can* speak. In eight different languages. I've traveled the seas of the world, you see. But I'm not getting any younger, and I've decided to settle down."

"And he does fine out of water," Rex added.

"A swim a day is all I need," Horatio agreed.

"He could teach the boys languages," Xenos said thoughtfully. "And how to dive."

Zara gave him a look that suggested she was questioning his sanity.

Something suddenly occurred to Beatrice. "Horatio, you must know the waters of the bay very well," she said.

Horatio slowly nodded his ponderous head. "I do."

"Then maybe you could help us."

"We need to find a way to get from the sandbar beyond the firedrakes to Ailsa's island," Ollie said.

"That won't be easy," the sea turtle replied, "with the sea monsters and all. I'm too old to outswim them anymore. That's one reason I've decided to retire."

"There must be *some* way," Beatrice insisted.

Horatio sat very still, appearing to be lost in thought. "Perhaps," he said at last. "There's a little boat on the sandbar, but it was abandoned there long ago. I'm not sure it would still float. And some of the sea monsters are so large, they could gobble it up in one bite."

Beatrice glanced at Ollie. "If the water were *boiling*," she said, smiling as the idea began to form in her mind, "that would take care of the sea monsters."

Ollie saw where she was going. "Yeah! And we'd be in the boat so the water wouldn't burn us."

"But the boat might sink," Cyrus reminded them.

"And it might not," Teddy said stubbornly. "We have to try it."

"If you can make it to the ring of sand that surrounds the Island on the Edge," the sea turtle said, "I know some sea horses who will help you. Rosebud and Percy. They're old friends of mine. But getting to the island is only part of it," he went on. "Then you'll have scorpions to contend with—not to mention that giant sea serpent Hissyfit."

Beatrice nodded, feeling a little less confident. "We know. But we'll just have to deal with them when we get there."

Zara looked worried. "When are you leaving?" she asked Beatrice.

Beatrice glanced at her friends. "We probably shouldn't delay much longer. What about tomorrow?"

Ollie nodded. "Bridget said we'd have to leave at dawn."

"I'm going with you," Quincy said suddenly. "I might be able to help you navigate the bay."

Teddy's face lit up, but then Beatrice said, "I'd like that, Quincy, only you might be more helpful here. Someone needs to watch Miranda and make sure she doesn't follow us. And Sasha. We can't be worrying about her."

A look of disappointment crossed Quincy's face, but he hid it quickly. "Of course," he said. "I'll watch Miranda for you and try to keep Sasha occupied."

"I wish you'd reconsider," Zara said. "At least wait a few days."

"Don't make it harder for them," Xenos said quietly. "They know what they have to do."

16

Through the Dragon's Eye

It was still dark the next morning when Beatrice, Teddy, Ollie, and Cyrus made their way up the beach toward the black tower. Cayenne ran ahead, apparently eager to begin their adventure.

Beatrice was muttering the spell she would need to recite when they found Ailsa. She was so preoccupied she didn't even notice Bridget until they were practically upon her. The bonfires out in the water cast a golden glow on the older witch's face. Perhaps it was only the flickering light, but Beatrice thought she saw an excited sparkle in her great-aunt's brown eyes.

"I've made a decision," Bridget said. "I'm going with you."

Beatrice was taken aback by this. Her first thought was that they couldn't afford to have someone along who would lose her nerve and put them all in jeopardy. Then Beatrice felt ashamed. Hadn't she herself been frightened both times they'd set out to break Dally Rumpe's spell?

Bridget was watching Beatrice with shrewd eyes. "I know what you're thinking," she said, "but I won't be a burden."

"I know you won't," Beatrice said quickly. And she realized that she couldn't deny Bridget this chance to redeem herself.

"We have a few minutes until the sun comes up," Bridget told them. "Let's stand over there, at the edge of the water. We'll hold hands and focus on the firedrake directly in front of us. When we see the dragon's eye, I'll count to three. Then we'll all jump at the same time, while we visualize ourselves leaping through the eye."

"Neat!" came a voice from behind them.

They all turned around to see a smiling Sasha standing there. Quincy was just behind her, looking apologetic.

Sorry. Quincy mouthed the word to Beatrice and shrugged sheepishly.

Sasha glanced around at Quincy and grinned. "He tried to stop me from coming," she said, "but I slipped out a side door. I promise not to get in your way! I just want to be there. *No one* else will have a first-person account of you reversing the spell."

As always, Beatrice wasn't too sure that they *would* be able to reverse the spell. And she was afraid the reporter was going to be nothing but trouble.

"Please, Beatrice," Sasha pleaded. "I need this job."

Beatrice nodded reluctantly. "Okay, as long as you realize it's going to be dangerous." Then she said to Quincy, "What about Miranda?"

"I didn't see her," Quincy replied.

"Me, either," Sasha said. "There was just Angel watching us from the window."

That caused Beatrice a moment of uneasiness. "What's he doing here this early?" she wondered aloud.

"He keeps strange hours," Quincy said. "Sometimes he comes to work at two or three in the morning. And look over there."

They all peered down the beach in the direction Quincy was pointing and saw Wadsworth Fretwell sitting on a sand dune. He looked up and started to wave.

"We should have sold tickets," Teddy muttered.

Bridget looked out over the water, where a ribbon of light had appeared along the horizon. "We'd better get into position," she said.

Beatrice picked up Cayenne and placed the cat on her shoulder, then walked with the others to the water's edge.

"Everyone hold hands," Bridget said.

Beatrice found herself clasping Bridget and Ollie's hands. She smiled at Ollie and he winked at her. Beatrice blew her bangs out of her eyes and stared at the bonfire in front of them.

"Do you see the dragon's head?" Bridget asked. "And the eye? Focus on the eye."

Beatrice concentrated hard on the shape the flames made. She could make out the head—and, yes, there was the dragon's eye. At first, it simply looked like a small hole in the flames. But as she stared into the hole, it suddenly turned a warm gold color—and seemed to take on a quivering life of its own!

"Is there anyone who doesn't see it?" Bridget asked. "Tell me now, because this won't work if you don't see it."

No one spoke.

"All right then," Bridget said softly. "I'm going to count to three. Focus, focus. On the count of three, stare into the eye and jump. One. Two. Three."

When Bridget said *three*, Beatrice bent her knees and leaped as high as she could into the air. She had the sensation that the ground was falling away—that she was flying! And the distant eye of the firedrake was suddenly in her face, huge, swirling, surrounded by flames. Then she was inside the flames herself, shooting through them. She felt an instant of terror, sure she was going to be burned. And then, abruptly, her feet hit something solid. She stumbled, and fell to her knees.

Beatrice looked around, feeling dizzy and confused. She realized that she was squatting on a narrow strip of sand far out in the bay, with the firedrakes behind her. Beatrice couldn't believe it. Bridget's idea of traveling through the dragon's eye had worked!

Then Beatrice reassured herself that Cayenne was still perched on her shoulder, the cat's claws digging into her skin, and saw that the others were all crouched around her on the sand. Beatrice quickly counted heads, and let out a long breath. They had made it.

"*That* was certainly different," Teddy said cheerfully.

Beatrice looked at Bridget, who was standing quietly by herself staring out over the water toward Ailsa's island.

"You did it," Beatrice said softly to Bridget. "Your plan worked."

Bridget nodded, her face serene in the golden light that was spreading quickly from the horizon. Beatrice thought her great-aunt seemed to be standing taller.

"Hey!" Ollie called out. "There's the boat."

They all followed him to a spot at the end of the sandbar, where a large rowboat was half buried in the sand. Its paint was peeling and several boards in the bottom were buckled.

"I don't know about this," Cyrus murmured. "Do you really think it'll float?"

"Only one way to find out," Teddy said. She fell to her knees and started to dig the boat out of the sand.

Ollie, Quincy, and Sasha followed suit, but Beatrice didn't move. She and Bridget were looking out over the water.

The rocky peaks of Ailsa's island were still quite a distance away, but Beatrice could see that they were steep cliffs, and would be hard—if not impossible—to climb. She hoped they wouldn't need to. And the narrow ring of sand that encircled the island was clearly visible from here. Then Beatrice noticed dark shadows beneath the water. As she peered closer, she could see that the bay was literally alive with swimming creatures. And she had a pretty good idea that these weren't fish she was seeing.

All of a sudden, something leaped up out of the water about twenty feet away. It was the size of a large dolphin, but this was no dolphin! The creature was dark and scaly, with dozens of razor-sharp fins down its back. As it left the water, it opened its huge mouth and Beatrice could see rows of long teeth that looked like daggers.

Beatrice staggered back, holding tightly to Cayenne, and Bridget reached out a steadying hand.

"This is what we have to get past?" Beatrice whispered as she watched the monster hit the water with a splash and disappear beneath its surface.

The splash caused the others to look up from their digging.

"What was that?" Teddy demanded.

"This huge, horrible—*thing!*" Beatrice said. Her entire body was trembling.

They all stood up and stared out over the bay.

"Oh, gosh, look at that," Sasha said in a horrified whisper.

A creature that was at least ten feet long, black and snakelike, slithered through the surf that lapped against the sandbar. And it was only a few yards from where they stood!

Sasha squealed, then she and Cyrus leaped into the grounded boat.

"Can it come up on the sand?" Teddy asked.

"I don't know," Ollie answered. Although he sounded calm, Beatrice could see beads of sweat on his forehead. "But we'd better get this boat free. *Now!*"

Beatrice and Bridget ran to help, and before long they were sliding the rowboat into the water. Imagining all the horrors swimming nearby, Beatrice was careful to stay on the sand. She noticed that Sasha had pulled her notebook out and was scribbling furiously, even though the reporter looked pale and scared.

"Okay, everybody in," Quincy said.

They all piled into the boat, and Quincy reached for the oars. "We'll take turns," he said. "Who else wants to be first?"

"I will," Ollie replied.

Quincy pushed off with one of the oars, just as Beatrice saw a creature speeding through the water toward the boat. It had a fishlike tail, but its head was vaguely human—except for the hooked horns sprouting from its forehead and its long fanged snout. It was close enough for Beatrice to see the vicious glint in its pale protruding eyes and the opening of its wide mouth as it prepared to attack.

"Ollie!" Beatrice screamed. "Do the spell."

Ollie began to chant:

> *Heat of flame, heat of fire,*
> *Give to me my one desire.*
> *Boil this water, bubbling free,*
> *As my will, so mote it be!*

Instantly, the water surrounding the boat began to bubble. Then creatures started to leap from the boiling water, jerking violently in the air and emitting terrible screams, before falling back into the scalding waves.

While Quincy and Ollie rowed, the others stared in horrified fascination as hundreds of sea monsters flopped and flailed and screeched all around them. Then, suddenly, the bay was silent and perfectly still.

After a while, Beatrice noticed that Quincy and Ollie's arms were beginning to tremble with exhaustion. "I can take a turn," she said.

But just as Beatrice and Cyrus took up the oars, Teddy cried out, "The boat's leaking!"

Beatrice looked down at her feet and saw an inch of water standing in the bottom of the boat.

"There's a hole here in front," Ollie said. "It's coming in pretty fast."

Cyrus yelped and pulled up his feet. "It's really hot!"

Beatrice looked around frantically. "Ollie?"

"Keep rowing," Ollie told her. "We'll bail."

Steam encircled them like fog, soaking their hair and clothes. And now Beatrice could feel heat rising from the bottom of the boat around her feet and legs. She rowed faster, mechanically, her mind blocking out everything except the pull of the oars against the boiling water. Until, finally, the bottom of the boat scraped against something solid. Beatrice looked up and realized with relief that they had reached the ring of sand.

They scrambled out of the boat, and Ollie began to chant the spell to make the water stop boiling.

The ring of sand was actually a sandstone reef, with shallow caves carved out in its hard surface. Beyond the reef was a stretch of water no more than a hundred feet wide that encircled Ailsa's island like a moat. Smaller creatures swam through this water, but Beatrice suspected that they were as deadly as the ones that lived in the open bay.

"Well, there it is," Bridget said. "The Island on the Edge."

They stood silently, gazing across the moat at their intended destination. A deserted beach swept up from the water, then the land rose sharply into steep rocky cliffs at the center of the island. A small house built of golden sandstone stood at the base of the cliffs.

"That's where Ailsa is held captive," Bridget said softly.

"So how do we get there?" Cyrus asked. "The boat's no good."

"It beats swimming," Quincy responded, grimacing at the shadows moving through the water of the moat.

"What about those sea horses Horatio mentioned?" Teddy asked suddenly. "He said they'd be here."

Beatrice looked around. All she saw were sand and stone and water filled with horrible creatures.

"He must have been mistaken," Beatrice said, stroking Cayenne and hoping that she didn't sound as worried as she felt.

But Sasha voiced all their fears when she said hesitantly, "What if we're stuck out here? Forever?"

17

Island on the Edge

"Forever is a *long* time," came a tiny voice. Startled, Beatrice's head jerked in the direction of the voice, her eyes darting across the stony landscape in search of its source. The others were looking around, as well, but they didn't see anything.

"Down *here*," the voice directed.

Beatrice looked at the ground. Water filled some of the crevices in the rock, forming shallow pools. Beatrice noticed movement in one of the pools, and when she peered closer, she saw them—two sea horses no bigger than her foot! Except they weren't like the sea horses she had seen in aquariums. They actually looked like miniature horses, with black silky manes and reddish brown coats that gleamed in the sun. But instead of back legs, they had fanned tails like fish.

"You must be Rosebud and Percy," Beatrice said. "Horatio told us about you."

"We heard you mention him," the larger of the horses said. "I'm Percy and this is Rosebud. So how can we help you?"

Everyone else had gathered around now, and they stooped down to look at the sea horses.

"We need to get to the Island on the Edge," Ollie said.

The sea horses exchanged a look. Then Rosebud said bluntly, "I don't know what we can do about that. You're all rather *large*."

"I can shrink us," Cyrus said eagerly. "Before you know it, we'll be three inches tall."

"Oh, well then," Percy said. "We could each carry one of you across to the island."

"Only one?" Teddy protested. "Couldn't you make several trips?"

"One trip is risky enough," Percy said, and then stared blandly at her as if to say, *Take it or leave it.*

"But how do you get past the sea monsters?" Beatrice asked.

Rosebud and Percy laughed, and it came out sounding like a soft whinny.

"We swim fast," Percy replied.

"We need to decide who'll go," Ollie said. "Beatrice, of course, since she has to recite the spell when she finds Ailsa."

"And who else?" Cyrus asked. He and Teddy looked hopefully at Beatrice. Ollie and Quincy tried hard not to.

"I don't suppose *I'll* be the one," Sasha said. Then she sighed. "No, it should be one of your friends."

"Or your family," Ollie said quietly.

Beatrice's eyes caught his. "Are you thinking what I'm thinking?"

Ollie smiled and shrugged. "It seems only fair."

Beatrice turned to Bridget and said, almost shyly, "Would you like to go with me to the island?"

Bridget blinked. "*Me?*" she asked, appearing stunned. "You want *me* to go?"

"You don't have to," Beatrice answered. "I just thought—well, you've worked so hard to protect the witches of Sea-Dragon Bay, I think you deserve to go. But don't feel obligated," she added quickly, realizing that Bridget might be afraid.

"I'm honored," Bridget said quietly. "And if you're sure you want me . . ."

"Very sure," Beatrice said firmly. Then she looked into the disappointed faces of her friends. But they were all smiling at her and nodding. Even Teddy. They understood that this short journey across the water to Ailsa's island would mean more to Bridget than it ever could to them.

"You guys are the best," Beatrice said softly.

"Well, let's get on with it," Cyrus said. "Are you ready?"

"Ready," Beatrice answered. She handed Cayenne to Ollie. "You'd better wait here, Cay. You never did care much for water."

"Don't worry," Ollie said. "We'll take good care of her."

Holding Bridget and Beatrice's hands, Cyrus began to chant:

> By the mysteries, one and all,
> Make them shrink from tall to small.
> Take them down to inches three,
> As my will, so mote it be!

Beatrice felt that strange sensation of being sucked down a drain, swirling around and around and around. When her head stopped spinning, she realized that she was standing shoulder to shoulder with Percy and Rosebud. And with Bridget, who looked astonished.

"This is amazing," Bridget said, shaking her head. "I've never seen anyone do that before."

"It's getting pretty routine with us," Teddy replied.

Percy swam over to the edge of the pool. "Well, mount up," he said.

Beatrice climbed on his back and Bridget seated herself on Rosebud.

"Grip our necks tightly," Rosebud said. "Oh, and we should warn you—we'll have to go under water to get out of here."

"Be careful," Ollie said gravely to Beatrice.

"We'll be waiting for you," Cyrus said.

"Don't forget any of the details," Sasha added.

"Hold your breath," Percy told them.

With their friends looking on and waving farewell, Beatrice felt the sea horse's sudden plunge beneath the water. It felt like taking a steep drop on a roller coaster, except that Beatrice couldn't scream while holding her breath and everything was green and shadowy. But the sea horse moved swiftly, and in less than a minute, Percy had surfaced in the water beyond the ring of sand. Beatrice shook her wet hair out of her face and saw a drenched Bridget clinging to Rosebud's neck.

"Stay safe," Teddy called.

But before Beatrice could respond, the sea horses had taken off toward the island.

With only their heads above water, Beatrice could feel the press of the water against her body as the sea horses sliced through it with amazing speed. It would have been an exhilarating ride if Beatrice hadn't been so worried about what was swimming around them. Then she saw a dark body the size of a large shark just a few feet away. And it was heading for them!

"Percy!" Beatrice screamed. "Something's after us."

She could feel the sea horse speed up, and then Percy tore past the creature. But there were more ahead.

Beatrice caught sight of a long serpentine body stretched out in front of them. *We're going to run right into it,* she thought in horror. But the next thing Beatrice knew, Percy was leaping into the air and sailing over the reptile. They hit the water with a splash on the other side. As Percy accelerated, Beatrice peered over her shoulder and saw Rosebud and Bridget land just behind Percy.

They were getting close to the island now, and Beatrice was holding her breath. "Just a few more yards," she whispered. "Let us make it, let us make it, let—"

Beatrice froze when she saw what appeared to be a whole family of sea serpents floating on top of the water just ahead. Then she realized that all those long twisting bodies were joined to a hideous lump of slimy pink flesh. *Was it an octopus?* In her miniaturized state, the creature looked as big as a house.

The octopus's tentacles were reaching out to grab the sea horses, coming within inches of Beatrice's face, when Percy and Rosebud said at the same time, "Hold your breath!"

The sea horses dove, and it felt to Beatrice that her stomach had been left behind. She was holding onto Percy's neck for dear life, feeling dizzy from lack of oxygen and afraid she was going to be sick. It didn't take much thought for Beatrice to understand that she was in trouble. If Percy didn't come up in the next few seconds, Beatrice knew she would drown.

And then, just when she felt that her chest was going to burst, the sea horse broke through the surface of the water. Beatrice threw her head back and gasped for air. She saw Bridget on Rosebud's back doing the same.

"Time for you to leave us," Percy said.

"*What?*" Beatrice looked around in confusion and realized that they were very close to shore. *They had reached the Island on the Edge.*

"It's been a pleasure," Rosebud said, "but you really must get off now."

"We can't tarry," Percy added, "unless you want us to be some sea monster's dinner."

Beatrice and Bridget slid off the horses' backs. Since they were only three inches tall, the water came up to their shoulders.

"Go on," Percy directed. "We'll wait until you reach the beach."

Beatrice and Bridget began to swim. Soon they were dragging themselves from the water onto the warm golden sand.

"Good luck!" Percy called. And then the sea horses took off in the direction of the ring of sand.

"Thank you, thank you!" Beatrice and Bridget stood on the beach, still breathing heavily, and waving until the sea horses were out of sight.

Then Beatrice turned around and looked across the wide expanse of sand to the house at the foot of the cliffs. Bridget started toward the house, but Beatrice caught her arm.

"It's never that easy," she said softly. "I don't see anything, but I'm sure that giant sea serpent is somewhere nearby."

"Hissyfit," Bridget said.

Beatrice nodded. "Why don't we go over to that pile of rocks at the base of the cliffs? We can hide and watch the house for a while from there."

They started across the sand to the rocks. But they were so small, progress was slow and Beatrice felt vulnerable out in the open. She looked around uneasily and that's when she noticed something out of the corner of her eye. Something *moving*.

Beatrice spun around and saw a creature at least four times her size crawling through the sand toward them. It was black, with eight skinny legs, giant claws, and a curved tail. A scorpion! Dr. Meadowmouse's warning flashed through Beatrice's mind. *Their sting can kill.* Then Beatrice realized that this guy wasn't alone. More were coming up over a sand dune behind him. There were dozens—no, *hundreds*, Beatrice saw now—and she watched in horror as they spread out across the beach. With a sinking feeling in the pit of her stomach, she realized that the scorpions' movements were deliberate. They were surrounding Bridget and herself, leaving no opening for them to escape.

Bridget had seen the scorpions now, and she grabbed hold of Beatrice's arm. At first Beatrice thought the older witch was holding on to her for support. But then Bridget shoved her. *Hard!*

"Our only chance is to make it to the cliffs," Bridget said sharply. "*Run!*"

Beatrice didn't waste time with questions. She started running through the sand, with Bridget on her heels. She could hear a swishing sound behind her. Looking over her shoulder, Beatrice saw that the scorpions were coming faster now, their horrible legs kicking up sand as they skittered across the beach in pursuit of the two witches. When Beatrice and Bridget reached the base of the cliffs, the scorpions were less than a foot away.

"Start climbing," Bridget said.

Beatrice grabbed an outcrop of rock and pulled herself up. The side of the cliff was steep, and loose pebbles under her feet made it hard to keep her balance. And if she fell . . . Beatrice looked down, where an army of scorpions had gathered at the bottom of the cliffs. They were clicking their claws angrily and switching their venomous tails. If she fell, *they* would be waiting.

Beatrice and Bridget climbed for a long time. Sometimes they were forced to crawl on their hands and knees, the sharp rocks cutting painfully into their skin. Finally, her arms and legs aching with exhaustion, Beatrice paused to rest. But then she glanced down—and saw that some of the scorpions were climbing up the rocks after them. Beatrice forced her throbbing legs to start moving again.

While she climbed, Beatrice tried frantically to think of a way to escape. Even if they had been normal size, making it to the top of the cliffs would have been difficult. But in their current circumstances, Beatrice knew they would never be able to climb that far.

Then she saw a narrow ledge of rock not far above them and had an idea. If they could make it that far, they might be able to walk around the side of the cliff—and *maybe* find a safe way down on the other side.

Too weary to speak, Beatrice pointed to the ledge. Bridget nodded, seeming to understand. Meanwhile, more of the scorpions had started up the cliff after them.

Motivated by hope, Beatrice and Bridget moved more quickly. Beatrice's fingers were numb and she could no longer feel the pain in her bloodied hands. She just focused on the ledge and climbed—until she was able to reach up and touch it with her fingertips.

Bridget leaned against her, trying to smile. "We've almost made it," she said.

"You go first," Beatrice said. "I'll help you."

Bridget inched her way up the steep wall of rock, with Beatrice supporting her from below. The older witch finally managed to pull herself onto the ledge, where she collapsed.

"Are you okay?" Beatrice asked anxiously.

Bridget's face appeared over the edge. She was grinning. "I'm great," she said, and extended a hand down to Beatrice.

Bridget was stronger than she appeared. Holding on to Beatrice's hands, she tugged, while Beatrice braced her feet against the cliff and moved slowly up its side. When Beatrice's face was even with Bridget's, she hooked her elbows over the ledge and lifted herself to the shelf of rock.

They sat there for a few moments, breathing hard and feeling giddy with a shared sense of accomplishment. Then Beatrice looked down. The scorpions hadn't given up, but they were still some distance below the ledge.

Staggering to her feet, Beatrice said, "We'd better get moving."

And that's when she saw them. Four men were standing on the ledge about ten feet away, leering at Beatrice and Bridget. From Beatrice's three-inch perspective, the men appeared huge, not to mention filthy and dangerous.

They had tangled beards and wore ragged coats and breeches. Brightly colored scarves were tied around their heads, and one had a gold ring hanging from his earlobe. The man in front was holding a sword, its long blade flashing in the bright sunlight.

Beatrice suddenly remembered Dr. Meadowmouse saying that there were cutthroat pirates on the island. She glanced quickly at Bridget and was surprised to see that the older witch was staring at the pirates without apparent fear.

The pirate with the sword moved toward them. His dark eyes glistened as he looked at Beatrice, making her skin crawl.

"So what have we here," the pirate boomed. "Could it be two tiny witches?" He glanced at his companions. "What'll we do with 'em, mates? Toss 'em to the scorpions?"

"*Too easy!*" one of the other pirates bellowed. "Make 'em walk the plank."

"Now you're talking," a third pirate said. "We'll feed 'em to the sea monsters!"

The pirate with the sword turned back to Beatrice and Bridget, grinning horribly so that they could see his rotted teeth. "You heard the maties," he said in a voice that was chillingly matter-of-fact. "I guess your goose is cooked."

18

Hissyfit

Beatrice and Bridget found themselves scooped up in the lead pirate's dirty hand and stuffed without ceremony into the pocket of his coat. When the pirates began their descent from the cliffs, Beatrice could feel every step they took. She was jostled and tossed and thrown against Bridget until her body was bruised and aching.

Finally, they were on level ground, and Beatrice was able to stand. She reached up to see if they could slip out of the pocket, but the flap was apparently buttoned shut. Beatrice sat down beside Bridget to think. *If only I had scissors to cut through the fabric*, she thought. *Or a match to catch his pocket on fire*. Beatrice smiled grimly. *That* would make him take off his coat quick enough.

Then she heard Bridget whisper, "Are you afraid?"

"Terrified," Beatrice admitted.

"Me, too," Bridget said.

"Are you sorry you came?" Beatrice asked, feeling very sorry herself that she had suggested Bridget come with her.

"Certainly not," Bridget whispered promptly. "I've felt more alive today than I have in forty years." Bridget squeezed Beatrice's shoulder. "And it isn't over yet, you know."

About that time, Beatrice realized that the pirate was walking uphill, and the soft sounds his boots made against the sand had changed to dull thuds. *We must be going up the ramp to their ship*, Beatrice thought. Then a hand suddenly dipped into the pocket and lifted them out roughly. Clutched tightly in the curl of calloused fingers, Beatrice could see that they were on an old-time ship like she had seen in movies. Tall masts loomed over them, with the sails rolled up. Beatrice looked around to get her bearings, but all she could see were the cliffs rising on one side of the ship and open water on the other side. Since there was no sign of the sandbar or the firedrakes, Beatrice assumed they were on the far side of the island.

The pirates were talking in loud voices, but their words were drowned out by bursts of menacing laughter. Beatrice and Bridget were being taken across the deck to the other side of the ship. The pirate carrying them stepped up and Beatrice saw a narrow board extending out over the water. Her heart lurched and then started to pound. He was taking them to the end of the plank!

The pirate stooped and opened his hand. Beatrice and Bridget tumbled out and hit the wood. Beatrice fell on her arm and felt a wrenching pain in her shoulder. She glanced over to see if Bridget was all right and saw the older witch staggering to her feet. She thought Bridget looked angry. *Good for her*, Beatrice thought, feeling pretty mad herself.

Beatrice stood up, ignoring the pain in her arm. She could see now that they were only a few inches from the end of the plank. The pirate's booted feet blocked them from running back to the deck of the ship, and below them was nothing but blue-green water.

Beatrice forced herself to look down into the water. There were more shadows than she could count beneath the surface, dark monstrous bodies circling around and around directly below the plank. The deadly creatures seemed to sense that they were in for a treat. Within the swarming mass, Beatrice could pick out the slithering shapes of serpents and the greedy gaping mouths of other beasts, all waiting restlessly for whatever would fall from the plank.

The pirate placed the tip of his sword against the wood at Beatrice's feet. "You first," he said. And then, "Walk!"

Behind them, the other pirates cheered and roared with laughter.

Beatrice turned to see Bridget's face, which was pale and strained, but the dark eyes blazed. Beatrice marveled. Even now, with no possibility of escape, Bridget hadn't given in to despair. Her courage was contagious. Beatrice looked up at the pirate and didn't move.

The pirate made an angry noise in his throat. "Walk!" he shouted, and pushed the blade of the sword against her back.

Beatrice took one step and stopped. The waters beneath her had grown turbulent with the frenzied movement of the sea monsters. Beatrice's eyes were drawn down to the predators. Then she felt the cold steel of the sword against her back again as the pirate prodded her on.

"We don't have all day," he said roughly. "Move!"

Beatrice took another step. She was so close to the end of the plank, she could look over it and see the churning water below. *One more step*, she thought, and her knees threatened to buckle.

Beatrice felt the nudge of the sword again, and knew that this was it. But then she heard scuffling noises behind her and looked over her shoulder to see what was happening. There was Bridget facing the ship, and the pirate bounding up the plank toward the deck. Beatrice felt relief, as well as total bewilderment. Why was he running? Then she noticed the other pirates scurrying across the deck, no longer laughing, but yelling and grabbing for buckets. That's when she saw the smoke. And the flames! Fire was shooting up from the deck along one of the masts.

"Come on!" Bridget shouted. She grabbed Beatrice's hand and pulled her toward the ship.

They ran up the plank and leaped down to the deck. The pirates were all running around, spilling water and dropping buckets in their haste, and swearing and snarling at one another. Beatrice and Bridget stayed close to the railing to avoid being stepped on and made it to the ramp without being seen.

The pirates were still falling all over one another to put out the fire as Beatrice and Bridget sped down the ramp to shore. Beatrice looked back when her feet hit the sand and saw that the pirates hadn't even missed them.

When Beatrice and Bridget reached the rocks at the foot of the cliffs, Beatrice said, "I think we need to go that way," and pointed west.

Bridget nodded, and they took off.

They stayed close to the cliffs, hidden among the piles of rock and scraggly bushes, hoping they would end up on the shore side of the island again. After placing some distance between themselves and the pirates, Beatrice suggested they rest a few minutes.

Bridget sank to the ground and leaned back against a boulder. She looked at Beatrice and grinned. "Not bad for an old witch," she said in a sassy voice, "even if I do say so myself."

Beatrice laughed. "You're amazing," she said simply.

"I think we make a pretty good team," Bridget answered.

Beatrice's brow furrowed as her thoughts returned to the pirates. "Were we just lucky," she asked suddenly, "or was that fire more than a coincidence?"

A smile tugged at Bridget's mouth. "Remember what I told you, Beatrice? I can start fires. With the blink of an eye," she added.

Beatrice sat straight up. "It was *you*?" Then she started to laugh, and Bridget joined in.

Thirty minutes later, the roof of Ailsa's house came into view. Across the water was the sandbar, and far in the distance they could see the flames of the firedrakes.

Beatrice's eyes darted back to the house. "Let's go closer," she said.

They crept along the base of the cliffs.

"I don't see anything—" Beatrice started, and then the words died in her throat. Because coiled around the foundation of the house was the most appalling sight she could imagine—a serpent so long that it had managed to wrap itself all the way around the house!

Beatrice stood paralyzed, not wanting to look but unable to tear her eyes away. The sea serpent's body was as thick as a man was tall, its copper-brown scales shimmering in the sunlight. And the massive wedge-shaped head was especially horrible, held erect and swiveling slowly as the creature's glittering eyes scanned the landscape like some sort of hideous spotlights. The head turned in their direction, and Beatrice shuddered.

"I can't do it," she said softly. But even as she spoke, Beatrice hated the sound of those words! After all she and her friends had faced, how could she think of backing out now? But the serpent—this Hissyfit!—was just too much. How could they hope to fight a monster that terrible?

"I wouldn't even know how to begin," Beatrice muttered.

"It does seem overwhelming," Bridget agreed. "But there might be a way."

Beatrice raised her head and looked at Bridget with dull eyes. She didn't want to hear this. She wanted her great-aunt to concede that it was impossible!

"I told you that I have two talents," Bridget said. "You've seen the first one."

Beatrice nodded. "Starting fires."

"And the second," Bridget said calmly, "is charming snakes."

Beatrice cut her eyes at Bridget and frowned. "That thing isn't exactly your ordinary snake," Beatrice said, but Bridget had her attention now. "You said that you and Uncle Xenos used to catch *garter* snakes."

Bridget shrugged. "A difference in size is all."

Beatrice nearly laughed, except the situation was too grave. She was feeling ashamed because she wanted to forget this whole Dally Rumpe business and go home. And she was also feeling cranky—because she *couldn't* go home. There was no way off this awful island unless she and Bridget reversed Dally Rumpe's spell. And even if they could leave, she'd never be able to live with herself if she didn't at least try to help Ailsa.

Beatrice sighed. "Okay," she said. "What do we do?"

"I need to get closer to him," Bridget said. "And, of course, he'll have to be able to see me."

Beatrice looked into her great-aunt's determined face. *This* was the woman who called herself a coward?

"I just want to tell you," Beatrice said, "no matter what happens, I think you're the bravest person I've ever met."

Bridget placed her hands on Beatrice's shoulders and said, "I've been thinking the same thing about you."

Beatrice was feeling some pretty strong emotions, but she didn't have time to give in to them. Bridget was already straightening her robes and squaring her shoulders, preparing to step out to meet the foe.

Beatrice scrambled after her, and they emerged from behind the rocks together. Hissyfit saw them immediately, but the serpent didn't move. His coppery eyes just followed their progress as they walked slowly toward him.

"Do you remember what to do?" Beatrice whispered anxiously. "It's been a long time."

"I remember," Bridget replied.

When they were only a few yards away from the giant serpent—just out of striking distance, Beatrice hoped—Bridget said loudly, "You must be Hissyfit. I've come to sing you a song."

The sea serpent cocked his flat leathery head to one side, as if her words surprised him. Then he snapped his head erect and the hooded eyes glowed with malevolent pleasure. Beatrice could almost hear the snake thinking, *Let her sing, if she wants. I'll eat the other one first.*

Bridget began to sing, but the words made no sense to Beatrice. She wasn't even sure they were words at all, because the sounds Bridget was making were more like the high-pitched wail of some strange musical instrument. And Beatrice realized with a sudden gnawing in her stomach that the sounds didn't seem to be working. Hissyfit was heaving his monstrous body away from the house. And still staring at them with his piercing eyes, he started to slither toward them.

Beatrice stifled a scream, but Bridget just stood there and continued to make those peculiar sounds.

The serpent moved closer, his powerful body coiling across small dunes of sand and leaving them flattened. Beatrice's heart was pounding so hard, all she could hear was a roaring in her ears. It deafened her to Bridget's song and to the whisper of Hissyfit's scales as they rubbed against the sand.

Suddenly the serpent reared up, his head held taut, his eyes burning into their flesh—and Beatrice waited for the strike of his fangs. *Will it hurt?* she wondered, feeling strangely detached from what was happening.

But seconds passed, and the serpent didn't strike. Hissyfit was holding the same position, and then, astonishingly, his head began to sway gently from side to side.

Beatrice's eyes darted from the sea serpent to Bridget. She could see that her great-aunt was still singing, and as the pounding in Beatrice's ears lessened, she could hear the wailing tone of Bridget's voice. Beatrice looked back at Hissyfit and saw that the serpent was still swaying, moving rhythmically in time to Bridget's song.

Beatrice couldn't believe it. The music was working! She grabbed hold of Bridget's arm and began to edge toward the house.

The serpent was no longer blocking their way, but they would still have to pass frighteningly close to his body. It seemed to Beatrice that they were moving in slow motion, but she was afraid a sudden move would startle Hissyfit out of his trance. Gripping Bridget's arm tightly, Beatrice inched past the serpent's head, while Bridget continued to sing.

As they moved down the sea serpent's endlessly long body, the beast turned his head to follow them, still swaying. Then all of a sudden he lifted himself higher—and Beatrice drew in a sharp breath, certain he was going to lunge. But the serpent meant only to turn himself to follow the tantalizing music. His great body coiled again and he made a slithering move in their direction.

Every nerve in Beatrice's body leaped in alarm, but she forced herself to stay calm and move slowly. Finally, they reached the steps to the house. And to Beatrice's amazement, the front door opened.

"Come in," said an urgent voice from inside. "*Hurry!*"

At that moment, Hissyfit stopped swaying. Beatrice could see a flicker in the coppery eyes, and she knew the trance was broken. The serpent lowered its head toward Beatrice and Bridget, and with a forceful sweep of his tail, he struck.

19

Reunion

Beatrice and Bridget leaped inside. The serpent's spearlike fangs missed them by a hair and struck the door, splintering the wood. Hissyfit jerked his head back and spit out bits of wood, hissing in fury. He was about to lunge again when a young woman suddenly stepped out of the shadows and slammed the door in his face.

The woman turned to Beatrice and Bridget, staring down at them with wide blue eyes. Hair the color of pale sand spilled across the shoulders of her dark gold robes and halfway down her back. She took a step toward them and said in a resigned voice, "A door won't keep him out, you know."

"We're Bailiwick witches," Beatrice said hastily, "and we're here to break Dally Rumpe's spell."

"I'm Ailsa," the young woman said, her eyes opening even wider. Then color flooded her cheeks and her lips lifted into an astonished smile. "You've come to help me?"

"That's right," Beatrice said, "and I have to repeat the counterspell in your presence."

Then she began to chant:

> By the power of the east,
> By the beauty of the light,
> Release this circle, I do implore,
> Make all that's wrong revert to right.

Suddenly there was a loud cracking sound overhead and the house began to shake. Ailsa grabbed hold of the window frame to steady herself, but Beatrice and Bridget were thrown to the floor. To their small bodies, the vibrations felt like an earthquake.

They heard the terrifying sound of wood snapping and splitting apart. One wall started to shimmy and the floor buckled in the middle. Large pieces of plaster fell from the ceiling and crashed around them.

Beatrice was trying to scramble to her feet, but the shifting floor made it impossible to stand. Ailsa suddenly tumbled to the floor, and Beatrice looked out the window where the witch had been standing. She could see the heaving coils of Hissyfit's massive body pressed against the glass.

"He's wrapped himself around the house," Bridget said as she tried to crawl to Beatrice. "He's crushing it."

At that moment, two opposite walls broke in the center and lurched toward each other. More of the ceiling came crashing down. The house was literally caving in around them!

Glass in the windows began to shatter and Beatrice ducked beneath the sagging drapes to escape the falling shards. Bridget took cover under the fabric with her.

"If we were normal size, we might be able to get away through one of the windows," Beatrice said.

Ailsa pulled back the drapes and peered in. "*I'm* normal size," she said. "I could carry you."

"Maybe that won't be necessary," Beatrice said quickly, and began to chant:

> By *the power of the east,*
> By *the spirit of the wood*—

At that moment, Beatrice glanced up at the ceiling and saw that the support beams were cracking.

"We have to get out!" Beatrice shouted.

In an instant, Ailsa had picked up Beatrice in one hand and Bridget in the other, and was stepping up into the window. Her robes caught on jagged pieces of glass in the frame. She pulled the robes loose and looked down, preparing to jump. Then she saw the brown-and-copper scales of the sea serpent as he squeezed the foundation of the house.

Ailsa hesitated, teetering precariously on the window ledge.

"He can't see you," Beatrice said hastily. "His head must be on the other side of the house. When you jump down, can you miss him?"

Ailsa appeared terrified, but she nodded. Then she flung herself out the window! As they sailed toward the sand, Beatrice chanted hurriedly:

> Release this circle, I do implore,
> Make all that's evil, revert to good.

When Aisla hit the ground, Beatrice felt the jolt from her toes to the top of her head. She shook her head to clear it and looked up at the house—just in time to see the roof come crashing down. It made a thunderous noise, and the air was filled with dust and flying debris.

"Go to the cliffs!" Beatrice shouted.

Ailsa began to run. From the witch's clenched fist, Beatrice could see coil after coil of glittering scales emerge from the heap of broken wood and stone. The leathery head swiveled in their direction and the copper eyes spotted them. Hissyfit whipped around and started after them.

Ailsa looked back as she started up the steep cliff wall and saw the serpent slithering with alarming speed across the sand toward them. She tried to climb faster, but Beatrice knew they couldn't outrun him. And there wasn't time to finish the counterspell. In desperation, Beatrice began to chant:

Circle of magic, hear my plea,
Bring a tidal wave in from the sea
To sweep away this enemy,
While guarding the safety of my friends and me.
As my will, so mote it be!

Ailsa had stopped climbing and was now staring down at Beatrice in bewilderment. Then her eyes shifted to the serpent, who had started up the cliffs and was gaining ground.

As Ailsa's face registered panic, Beatrice had time to utter one word. "Look!"

Ailsa turned toward the bay, where a wall of water at least twenty feet high surged toward the island. With a deafening roar, the tidal wave swept across the beach, covering the sand and the rubble of Ailsa's house. Then the wave struck the cliffs.

The water rose so fast, and there was so much of it, Beatrice felt a moment of panic herself—until she realized that the top of the wave had hit below the spot where Aisla was standing. But the impact was powerful enough to make the cliffs tremble.

The wave receded as quickly as it had come, sweeping everything in its path out into the bay. Beatrice realized with relief that the sea serpent was nowhere to be seen. The tidal wave had carried him away, and he was out there, somewhere, under all that water.

Ailsa sank down weakly and opened her hands so that Beatrice and Bridget could step onto the rocks. Ailsa looked at Beatrice in awe. "You're a very powerful witch," she said solemnly.

Beatrice grinned. "Not even close!" she exclaimed, feeling giddy with relief.

"Come now," said a voice just above their heads. "Don't be so modest."

Beatrice's head jerked up. When she saw who was standing there, she felt a moment of confusion. Then she realized that it all made sense. There was only one way this witch could be on the island.

Sasha Leake raised her eyebrows and smirked. "You know who I am, of course," she said jauntily. "And you thought all along that *Miranda* was Dally Rumpe! She's awful," Sasha said with a grin, "but not *that* awful."

Bridget was standing with her hands on her hips looking up at Sasha in consternation. "But Dally Rumpe is a man!"

"I can take any identity I choose," Sasha boasted. "Too bad you didn't leave well enough alone, Bridget Bailiwick. You were right forty years ago when you decided that Dally Rumpe was too powerful an adversary."

Bridget just sniffed and turned her face away.

The dismissal enraged Sasha, and her expression turned ugly. Beatrice knew what to expect next. She had seen it once before. As Beatrice watched, the Sasha Leake mask began to crumble. The soft rounded face started to grow longer and more skeletal. The pink skin faded to a grayish pallor, and then stretched tightly across the angular cheekbones and square jaw until the sorcerer's face resembled a skull. Only the eyes appeared to be alive. Even sunken as they were now in their deep bony sockets, the eyes glittered with whatever demonic force drove Dally Rumpe. Beatrice was staring into a face that looked barely human. And then she remembered: This evil monster was a Bailiwick.

Beatrice forced her eyes to stay on that terrible face. "I've just learned that you and I are related," she said. "We're family."

The flash of fury in Dally Rumpe's eyes made Beatrice flinch. "I have no family," the sorcerer hissed.

Beatrice knew that she was probably being impossibly naive. Talk of family wasn't going to ignite any warmth in Dally Rumpe's frozen heart. But what did she have to lose?

"I've never wanted to hurt you," Beatrice went on doggedly. "If you'd reverse the spell yourself, and let your brother and his daughters go—"

Dally Rumpe threw back his head and laughed. Then he simply stared at her, his dark eyes smoldering. "Just like that," he said softly. "Turn over what's rightfully mine to that fool Bromwich. I'm afraid you've misjudged me."

Beatrice decided to try another course. "I understand why you're so angry with your father and brother. They didn't treat you fairly at all."

Dally Rumpe's eyes narrowed as he considered what she had said, then he seemed to catch himself and bellowed, "I don't have time for this chatter! Are you and this old witch going to make it easy? You can either walk off the cliff yourselves or I'll kick you off."

Neither Beatrice nor Bridget responded. But Beatrice cut her eyes to the side and realized that they were standing right on the edge. One boot of his foot and they'd be gone.

Dally Rumpe made an impatient sound in his throat and stepped toward them. Beatrice and Bridget jumped aside, but Beatrice stumbled and fell flat. The sorcerer's huge shadow cut out the sunlight as he bent down to finish her off.

When he reached for her, Beatrice saw that his fingers had changed into long hooked claws. With a sharp intake of breath, Beatrice tried to crawl away from those hideous talons—and backed into the solid rock wall.

"Let's be done with this," Dally Rumpe said. "There's no one to save you this time."

Just then, a loud voice said, "Let her go!"

Dally Rumpe stood up and spun around. He looked nearly as surprised as Beatrice felt when she saw the girl standing there glaring at the sorcerer.

Miranda Pengilly. Beatrice's eyes traveled up the girl's long white dress to the tangle of silver necklaces that fell to her waist, and she had the strangest sensation. It was as if they had been transported back in time—and Beatrice was seeing Miranda as she had appeared that first day at school. Her cousin was still beautiful and arrogant. *And brave*, Beatrice thought suddenly. Miranda was confronting the fearsome Dally Rumpe without a hint of apprehension in her pale gray eyes.

But how did she get here? And then Beatrice realized that she had been right all along. Miranda must have special entry to the island. She had to be working with Dally Rumpe!

Now the sorcerer's surprise turned to anger. "What did you say?" he demanded.

"I said," Miranda replied in a hard measured voice, "let her go. Bridget, too. You've shown them that they can't hurt you. They'll leave and never bother you again."

Miranda and Dally Rumpe's eyes locked in open warfare. "I thought you were the one Bailiwick with backbone," he said coldly. "That's why I agreed to let you help me. But I see now that you're as weak as the rest of them."

Miranda's silver eyes turned to ice. "You're the weak one. Nothing but a bully!" She spat the words at him. "I made a mistake getting involved with you."

Beatrice was fascinated by this exchange, but she knew that Miranda wouldn't be able to hold Dally Rumpe off forever. And meanwhile, Miranda was buying them valuable time.

Beatrice edged cautiously over to Ailsa. When Ailsa looked down, Beatrice motioned for the witch to pick her up. Ailsa glanced at Dally Rumpe—who was now accusing Miranda of betraying him—and bent down to scoop Beatrice up in her palm.

Beatrice began to chant softly, so that only Ailsa could hear:

> By the power of the east,
> By the chant of witch's song,
> Release this circle, I do implore,
> Make all that's weak revert to strong.

Miranda cut her eyes at Beatrice, then looked away quickly. She began to shout at Dally Rumpe, and Beatrice had the distinct feeling that Miranda knew exactly what Beatrice was doing.

> By the power of the east,
> By the goodness of the dove,
> Release this circle, I do implore,
> Make all that's hateful revert to love.

"You've become my enemy," Dally Rumpe snarled at Miranda. "You can join your dear family in their dive off the cliff!"

Dally Rumpe made a forceful move toward Miranda and she stumbled backward. Her heels were at the very edge of the cliff when Beatrice chanted:

> Heed this charm, attend to me,
> As my word, so mote it be!

Miranda finally looked afraid as the sorcerer took another step toward her. He reached for her and Miranda blinked.

"Your hand," she said softly.

Dally Rumpe looked down at his clawed hand and saw that it was beginning to evaporate. He whirled around to Beatrice, his expression more furious than she had ever seen it. And his eyes, glittering black in their deep sockets, were the eyes of a madman.

Beatrice steeled herself for whatever threat Dally Rumpe would fling at her, but the sorcerer suddenly fell to the ground. He writhed in pain against the rocks, shrieking in rage and disbelief, while his eyes searched for her. Knowing that he was beyond harming her or anyone else, Beatrice still shivered as those eyes came to rest on her. She thought she could actually feel the cold hatred that radiated from them.

Then Dally Rumpe's eyes rolled back into his head. His body began to blur, until all that remained of the sorcerer was a swirl of mist. They all watched silently as the mist drifted out across the bay, where it disappeared.

Beatrice looked down at the water. There were no dark shadows beneath its surface, no monsters leaping up from its depths. There was only beautiful turquoise water. Beatrice could almost see the tourists who would be coming back once they heard, to swim and fish and sail in the calm waters of Sea-Dragon Bay.

"How can I ever thank you?" Ailsa was asking.

"We should be thanking you," Beatrice said. "You got us out of the house before it caved in."

"And up to the cliffs," Bridget added.

Beatrice and Bridget exchanged a look and smiled at each other. "And *you* made all this happen," Beatrice murmured.

"Good grief!"

They all turned around at the sound of Miranda's voice.

Miranda was grimacing. "Are you people always this *nice?*" she demanded. "Are we going to sing campfire songs next? Pardon me while I go find my Mickey Mouse ears."

Beatrice grinned in spite of herself. "You'd better watch it," she warned. "*Nice* can be contagious."

"*Puh—lease*," Miranda responded, scowling at all of them.

"There's just one thing I don't understand," Beatrice said.

"Only one?"

Ignoring the sarcasm, Beatrice said, "If you were so determined to break Dally Rumpe's spell, why were you working with him?"

Miranda gave her a look that clearly said, *Surely you aren't that dense.* Then she said with a hint of pride, "So he'd trust me, of course. It's a lot easier to do someone in when they think you're on their side."

Well, that didn't work out too well, Beatrice thought.

They were silent for a moment, and then Beatrice said, "Miranda?"

"*What now?*"

"Thanks for saving our lives."

"Gag me," Miranda muttered.

But Beatrice had already turned to look out over the water toward the ring of sand. She could see them all standing there, waving—Teddy, Cyrus, Quincy, and Ollie with Cayenne on his shoulder.

Then Beatrice noticed the white Ghost Guard boat heading across the bay toward the island.

"Where were they when we really needed them?" Miranda grumbled. "Just tell me that."

20

The Last Firedrake

Darkness was gathering when Beatrice and her group returned to The Sandcastle. Lights glowed in every window. Banners had been hung above the door that read: *Welcome Home!* and *You've Made Us Proud!*

The Bailiwicks were waiting inside, and when Beatrice and Bridget led the way into the front hall, they all started to cheer and applaud. Then George opened the birdcages, and the hall was suddenly filled with swooping birds, while Rex made confetti rain down on everyone's head. Xenos and Zara settled for big hugs for the returning travelers, and Ulysses even managed to smile.

"Everybody's coming to the inn tonight," Zara said, beaming at them and weeping at the same time. "We're throwing the wildest party this town has ever seen."

"I'd like to freshen up first," Teddy said, running her fingers through her windblown curls.

"Of course," Zara said. "You'll all feel better after you shower and change." Then her eyes fell on Beatrice and Bridget's cut and battered hands. "And I'll call Dr. Cattermole."

Xenos came over to Bridget and looked at her for a moment, his eyes shining. "Are you all right?" he asked simply.

Bridget grinned. "More all right than I've been in years," she said.

Xenos laughed. Then he wrapped his arms around his sister and held her for a long time.

In the midst of all this joyful chaos, Beatrice noticed that Miranda was standing off to the side. She wasn't looking smug now; in fact, she actually appeared uneasy.

Xenos was watching Miranda, as well. He smiled gently at his granddaughter and said, "Welcome home, Miranda."

Miranda's face closed up and she nodded curtly.

The room had gone silent, and all eyes were fastened on Miranda and Xenos.

Beatrice felt a sudden urgent need to come to her cousin's defense. "She saved us from Dally Rumpe," Beatrice blurted out. "He had her backed to the edge of the cliff, but she kept him talking while I chanted the counterspell."

"So I've heard," Xenos said quietly.

Miranda frowned. "Then you've also heard that I was working with him," she said, some of her old arrogance resurfacing.

"That information did reach us," Xenos replied, his expression remaining impassive. "But helping your great-aunt and your cousin . . . well, that's a start."

Miranda was staring at him fiercely. "So what's going to happen to me?" she demanded.

"You'll be going away to school," Xenos replied briskly. "To The Rightpath School on the other side of the Sphere."

"Rightpath?" Miranda looked alarmed. "But that's a *reform* school!"

"Hardly," Xenos said. "Its academic program is one of the best in the Witches' Sphere."

"But it's for . . . for problem kids," Miranda sputtered.

"I think you qualify," Quincy muttered under his breath.

"They teach ethics and responsibility," Xenos said, "and they help talented young witches learn to use their gifts in a positive way."

"They have a waiting list," Zara pointed out. "You were lucky to be accepted."

"Right," Miranda said with a scowl. *"Lucky."*

"And you'll be safe there," Zara added.

Xenos nodded. "Since Dally Rumpe has no power in the mortal world, he can't come after Beatrice and her friends. But if you stay here, he *could* decide to take his fury out on you. There's strong magic to protect you at The Rightpath School, Miranda."

"And don't forget the locks and fences," Miranda muttered.

Xenos ignored that comment. "Once all this has died down—and we see that you've *really* changed," Xenos went on, a hint of sternness creeping into his voice, "you can come back here to live."

Xenos put an arm around Miranda's shoulders. "But you don't leave until tomorrow. And tonight, we're going to celebrate. You did a very brave thing today, Miranda, and you should be part of this."

Beatrice was surprised to see that Miranda didn't pull away. Instead, she lay her head on her grandfather's shoulder and sighed, as if the burden of being a very bad witch had taken its toll.

Everyone in town seemed to have gathered at The Firedrake Inn. As Beatrice and the others came through the door, they were greeted with thunderous applause. Then fireworks began to go off out over the water.

"The real kind," Quincy informed Beatrice with a grin. "But they don't hold a candle to what the Bailiwicks make when they're mad."

As they pressed through the crowd in the lobby, Beatrice scooped up Cayenne and placed the cat on her shoulder out of harm's way.

"You feel lighter," Beatrice said. "All this exercise has been good for you, Cay. Maybe you can afford to splurge on calories tonight."

"How about the salmon-spinach torte?" Quincy asked Cayenne, who responded with an emphatic *meow*.

Just then Beatrice noticed that Wadsworth Fretwell was standing behind the front desk. He was talking on the phone and appeared quite animated.

Beatrice glanced at Quincy, who shrugged.

Wadsworth hung up the phone, looking flustered and happy. "The phone hasn't stopped ringing," he declared. "Witches from all over the Sphere have heard that Sea-Dragon Bay is safe again."

As if on cue, the phone rang, and Wadsworth answered cheerfully, "Good evening. The Firedrake Inn. How may I help you?"

Beatrice turned quizzical eyes to Xenos.

"He works here now," Xenos said casually. "We needed more staff to handle all the reservations, and he's surprisingly good at it."

Quincy grinned at Beatrice. "You know Wadsworth. *He tries to be helpful.*"

Then Beatrice saw Kolliwobbles across the room. The pixie was juggling several flaming torches while balancing himself on a unicycle. A crowd had gathered around him, and his audience was clapping and laughing in appreciation.

"Don't tell me," Quincy said to his grandfather. "Kolliwobbles is going to entertain at the inn?"

"Well, no one else would hire him," Xenos said defensively. "And Kolliwobbles doesn't have to be a role model for this job—just amusing."

People were beginning to move outside to the deck that overlooked the bay.

"I almost forgot," Xenos said. "There's to be a ceremony before dinner. Come along, Bridget," he added, and took his sister's arm.

After living in seclusion for forty years, Bridget seemed nervous around so many people. "What is this, Xenos?" she asked anxiously.

"The firedrakes," Xenos said softly. "You can finally extinguish them."

A slow smile replaced the strained expression on Bridget's face. "I'll be happy to do that," she said.

The crowd parted and became silent as Xenos escorted Bridget to the edge of the deck. She stared out across the dark water at the leaping flames of the five firedrakes.

"You can come live with us now," Xenos said.

He looks happy, Beatrice thought. A terrible burden had been lifted from his shoulders, and it showed.

Bridget's eyes shifted to the black tower, barely visible now against the darkening sky except for the window at the top where a soft light burned.

"I've grown accustomed to my own home," Bridget said gently. She smiled at her brother. "Thank you for inviting me to live in the castle, but I think I'll stay where I am."

"But you're a hero," Xenos protested, "and the whole town is proud of you. There's no need to hide away any longer."

"No, there isn't," Bridget agreed. "And everyone is welcome to visit me. But the tower has been my comfort all these years. I don't see any reason to leave it now. And you have to admit, Xenos," she added, her eyes twinkling, "I have the best view in town."

"Put out the fires, Bridget," someone said. "We've had enough of them."

Xenos was nodding his agreement. Then he stopped, appearing thoughtful. "I wonder if we should keep one of them burning." He looked around at his friends and neighbors. "As a reminder of all we've been through. And to honor my sister—and these brave young people who risked their lives for Sea-Dragon Bay."

"That's a good idea, Xenos," said a voice in the crowd.

"The tourists will love it," came another voice, and Beatrice could hear the excited buzz of others agreeing.

Xenos turned back to his sister. "Are you ready then?" he asked.

"Am I ever! I've been waiting four decades to do this."

Then Bridget turned to Beatrice and held out her hand. "Come stand beside me, my dear. We'll do this together."

Beatrice came forward self-consciously, aware that hundreds of eyes were following her. But now they were friendly eyes.

Bridget took Beatrice's hand and held it tightly while she looked at the firedrake that was farthest away from them. Bridget blinked three times, and the bonfire went out. A collective sigh rose from those assembled, but no one spoke.

Bridget focused on the next bonfire, blinked, and the flames were extinguished. She put out a third fire, and then a fourth. Beatrice could feel the tension around her easing, and she expected the townspeople to burst out with shouts and applause. But they were silent, their eyes fastened to the lone bonfire that still burned, and Beatrice began to understand that this was a solemn moment for the witches of Sea-Dragon Bay. To them, the fires symbolized Dally Rumpe's tyranny, and all the pain they and their ancestors had suffered for two hundred years. It wasn't the time to scream and jump around, as witches are prone to do.

Beatrice noticed that Teddy and Quincy were standing nearby, talking too quietly for Beatrice to hear what they were saying. But the shy smiles on their faces said it all. Beatrice made a mental note: *Invite Quincy to visit us in the mortal world.*

About that time, Xenos came over and put his arm around Beatrice's shoulders. The look he gave her was tender.

"You've given my sister her life back," he said. "Come to think of it, you've given this whole town a future. And I don't know how—but I think you even managed to get through to Miranda. Beatrice, I want you to know," he went on, his voice gruff with emotion, "that I've never been more proud of the Bailiwick name than I am today. Along with everything else, you've given us our honor back."

Suddenly Zara stuck her head out the door and said in a loud excited voice, "The Witches' Executive Committee just arrived, and a Dr. Featherstone is asking for Beatrice. And Peregrine's come with them."

Teddy rolled her eyes. "You know what they're here to tell us," she said to Beatrice. " 'You're *so* brave—you're all to be commended—and by the way, we won't consider your classifications until you finish the rest of the test.' " Teddy made a face. "Have we been here before or what?"

"And they'll tell us about the next part of the test," Cyrus said. "What's the name of the place we go to after this?"

"Blood Mountain," Beatrice replied. "It's the western region of Bailiwick."

"Western?" Cyrus's face lit up. "Like with cowboys and horses?"

Beatrice laughed. "More like trolls and vampires, I'll bet."

"Come *on*," Zara said impatiently. "The committee's *waiting*."

Beatrice was eager to see Dr. Featherstone and Dr. Meadowmouse, and, of course, Peregrine. But as everyone else moved quickly inside, Beatrice lingered for a moment and stared out across the black waters of Sea-Dragon Bay. She wanted to see it one final time. The last firedrake.

Beatrice Bailey's Magical Adventures
By Sandra Forrester

Kids who loved *The Witches of Sea Dragon Bay* will enjoy
the first two adventures of Beatrice Bailey. Both stories are
a combination of fantasy, whimsy, and high adventure
guaranteed to keep young readers turning the pages.

The Everyday Witch
ISBN 0-7641-2220-7
Beatrice Bailey is tall, skinny, and about to turn twelve
years old. On that birthday she will get her official
classification as a witch. Will she be named an ordinary "Everyday Witch" or a specially empowered
"Classical Witch"? When the big day arrives, the
Witches' Executive Committee can't decide how to
classify her. At last, they agree that her Maximum Magic Level
must be tested, and to pass the test she must break a spell that has been cast by
the evil sorcerer, Dally Rumpe. Breaking the spell takes Beatrice and her three
best friends to several dangerous realms within the witches' sphere. In this tale,
their main challenge is to get past an enchanted hedge of thorns and a fire-
breathing dragon to undo the spell that has cast the land in snow and ice.

The Witches of Friar's Lantern
ISBN 0-7641-2436-6
In her second adventure, the Witches' Executive
Committee is continuing its test to see if Beatrice can
become a "Classical Witch," capable of working
important magic. She and her friends must now spend
time in the village of Friar's Lantern, a town surrounded by eerie swamps and located uncomfortably
close to a menacing neighboring village called
Werewolf Close. On a nighttime excursion they
encounter strange blue lights in the marshes. Further
bizarre adventures introduce Beatrice and friends to
a maddened old man witch named Yorick . . . a
weird group of magical cats . . . spooky ghosts who haunt the
swamps . . . and the toad-like water leaper, whose generous spirit belies his ugly
appearance.

Both Books: Paperback
$4.95, Canada $6.75

www.barronseduc.com

(#121) R7/03